Doctor Syn
on the High Seas

Black Curtain Press
PO Box 632
Floyd VA 24091

ISBN 13: 978-1-5154-2646-2

First Edition
10 9 8 7 6 5 4 3 2 1

Doctor Syn
on the High Seas

Russell Thorndyke

To the memory of John Buchan under whose auspices Doctor Syn was first published, I respectfully dedicate this volume, which completes the Doctor's history.

Prologue. The Syns o' Lydd

Syn is a name synonymous with "law and order" upon Romney Marsh. The Syns o' Lydd have been legal prolocutors and attorneys-at-law for Marshmen since the old days when Thomas Wolsey raised the lofty campanile of the parish church to heighten the glory of God in the neighbourhood, and incidentally to typify his own ambition. No doubt a Syn of those days was as useful to the Ipswich grazier's son as other Syns have been to native graziers upon the Marsh. Whenever they fell into legal difficulties there was always a Syn to pull them out.

So: an ancient town, Lydd; and an ancient race, the Syns.

Prolific, too, as their massed ranks of tombstones in the churchyard show; while their mural tablets in the church itself serve as a testimony for all time to the family's integrity and learning.

Go where you will in the neighbourhood, and rummage amongst old chests and cupboards until you have collected a pile of legal documents, ancient and modern, as high as Wolsey's Tower, and you will indeed be hard put to discover one parchment that does not show the signature of a Syn attorney.

Statutes, recognizances, fines, conveyance of land or messuage, recoveries, easements, vouchers, testaments and bequests—the signature of Syn appears upon them all.

Of comfortable means they always seem possessed. They inhabited the most mellow houses in Lydd and the adjacent New Romney. While waiting for clients, they purchased for themselves, until by judicious bargaining they gradually acquired much fertile land, large flocks of good wool, and such substantial homesteads that no other family could boast of a more delectable name upon the Marsh.

When there were no more purchasable properties upon the Levels of the Marsh, they lifted their eyes into the hills, carrying their territorial conquests along the sky-line from Aldington to Lympne. But when they realized that no financial embarrassment could shift the ancient Pemburys from their fastness of Lympne Castle, they pushed their own family possessions inland, acquiring property in Bonnington, Bilsington and Appledore, until there was even a Syn attorney secure in distant Tenterden, possessing the best cellars and stables in that comfortable sleepy town.

Now, the holding of land upon the hills gave to the Syns, as it did to other Marshmen in like case, a sense of security, for the reclaimed pasturage of Romney Marsh owed its existence to the Dymchurch Wall, which held the sea in check. The slogan of the Marsh, "Serve God, honour the King; but first maintain the Wall", showed that possible calamity was ever in their minds, and Marshmen liked to think they had a retreat in the uplands in the event of the sea breaking through and overwhelming the lower Levels. As folk in face of a common danger are apt to hang together, so did the Marshmen show a loyalty to one another. But none were so clannish as the Syns. They inter-married. Syn kith led Syn kin to the altar, and in due course added further cousins to the Syns. But just as in the most fruitful tree will sometimes have its barren period in all its branches, so did the Syn dynasty have its sterile age, and this in the mid years of the eighteenth century, the time in which this history is about to be unfolded. Then were the Syns sadly depleted. Jacobite tendencies caused the family to send their best blood to be spilled in the Young Pretender's cause.

Then an epidemic of ague which swept the Marsh took heavy toll, so that the Syns, who had in the past multiplied so exceedingly and covered the lands of the Levels of Romney, Welland, and Denge; the Syns who had covered as many dead sheepskins with ink as they had covered living sheepskins with wool, found themselves ten years after the "'45" bereft of their good men and true, and represented only by old Solomon Syn, attorney at Romney, and his nephew Christopher Syn, the youngest Don at Queen's College, Oxford, and the youngest Doctor of Divinity in either of the Great Universities.

His father, Septimus Syn, had been clerk to the Lords of the Level of Romney Marsh, under the magistracy of Sir Charles Cobtree, who resided at the Court House of Dymchurch-under-the-Wall. A tall, thin and austere man, this Septimus, who to all outward appearances was as dry as the parchments over which he toiled. But beneath his legal dustiness there must have burned a bright spark of adventurous romance, for at the outbreak of the "'45" he cast aside his quills and sandbox, buckled on his sword, and took ship to Scotland, where he joined the Young Pretender's force. He wisely left his wife and only child under the joint guardianship of his elder brother Solomon and Sir Charles Cobtree. Wisely, for with three of his brothers he was killed at Culloden. His wife followed him to the grave the same year—of a broken heart, it was said— and thus at the age of eighteen was Christopher Syn an orphan. Besides his two excellent guardians, his parents had bequeathed to him many other valuable assets: a sufficient sum of money to insure his independence and a brain and personality capable of improving with security.

In the year 1754, when this history begins, Christopher Syn was in his twenty-fifth year, and, as resident classical tutor at Queen's College, was respected by his elders and popular with his students. As his great friend Antony Cobtree told his father, Sir Charles, at Dymchurch, "I owe my degree to Christopher's patience and perseverance. By applying the spur at the right moment he lifted me over the hedges that barred my way to scholarship."

Although beloved by all, the young Doctor, two years junior to Tony Cobtree, was a sombre, tragic figure. Eyes deep, piercing and alive. Hair raven black. Tall, slim and weird, with a brooding melancholy that faded only when he smiled, and that because his smile conveyed a princely graciousness, and a pledge of loyal friendship to the fortunate recipient. Yes, a man of classic beauty and a strength well equipped to face and overcome whatever fate might hold in store for him. As an orator he was magnificent, for each spoken syllable claimed its utmost value, and every phrase its place of full significance, and backed in all its moods by expressive movements of his wonderful hands, whose strong delicacy could express more than most men's tongues. A personality that could not fail to make its mark in any walk of life, but was at present confined within the bounds of scholarship at Oxford University, a Doctor of Divinity. A priest. But more than all a man of high romance.

Chapter 1. Doctor Syn Meets Mister Mipps

On a misty morning of late September in the year 1754, young Christopher Syn, D.D., was riding along the flat top of the Dymchurch Sea-Wall in the direction of Lympne.

The Oxford Summer Vacation was drawing to its close, and he had spent it happily, partly with his uncle, the red-faced, rotund and jovial attorney at New Romney, and partly with his boon companion Tony Cobtree at Sir Charles' old Court-House at Dymchurch.The young student left the sea-wall and cantered his horse along the winding roads that crossed the Marsh. Eventually he reached the grassy bridlepath which runs along the foot of the hills, and has been made in years gone by for easy access from camp to camp by the Roman Legions. On either side the path sloped steeply down into deep, broad dykes, fed by the surface-water from the hills, but Syn's tall grey horse picked his way carefully. Meanwhile the sun, gathering strength, had dispersed the mist from the hills, and above him he could see his objective—the grim, frowning walls of Lympne Castle. He was on his way there to oblige Sir Henry Pembury, who had sent a Castle servant the night before to the Dymchurch Court-House, bearing a note requesting Doctor Syn to wait upon the Lord of Lympne at his earliest convenience. Being an old friend of his Uncle Solomon and a Justice of the Peace, the young cleric had taken the first opportunity to comply, though neither himself nor the Cobtrees could think why Sir Henry should thus summon him. Little did he imagine that such a simple journey was to be the prelude of a mighty Odyssey which would demand the abandonment of books and scholarship for murderous adventures with gunpowder and steel.

Opposite the Castle Hill, the bridle-path sloped gently down till level with the dyke-water, and it was here that a resolute horseman could save himself a good mile's detour by leaping the dyke. Knowing what was required of him, the horse, at the first touch of his master's heel, thundered down the slope, and with a sideways jump cleared the water with a good two foot to spare. Reining him in on the farther side, Doctor Syn patted the horse's neck and dismounted, and with the bridle over his arm led the way up the steep meadow that swept down from the Castle walls.

Throughout the ascent the man and horse threaded their way between giant blocks of crumbling masonry—all that was left of the great Roman Portus Lemanis. In some of these walls could yet be seen the metal rings for mooring galleys, but the grim bulwarks which had once held back the sea were now embedded in grass and used as shelter by the grazing sheep.

Now, bright noon-time, with sun-rays sparkling upon dewy grass-blades and a fine expanse of sea about one, is no time for a man to ruminate on ghosts, of things long dead, and yet Doctor Syn fell to wondering whether any Roman spectre yet mounted his guard in spirit form upon those walls.

Hardly had this flight of fancy flown to his brain when a sharp voice belonging to some invisible shape cried out the challenge, "Who goes there? I knows you. Halt and put your hands above your head." Doctor Syn halted, not so much from fear as from astonishment. He looked hard at the ruined bastion he was approaching, and from which the voice had issued, but could see nothing unusual.

"Now, then," went on the voice. "Hands up, I said and I don't see 'em up. No humbug now. I knows you and you knows me."

"Whom do you take me for?" asked Doctor Syn politely.

"For what you are, of course," came the indignant answer: "the new Riding Officer at Sandgate—grey horse and all, and dressed like an undertaker. Well, you won't undertake me, because I ain't a-going to be undertook." It was then that Doctor Syn noticed the brass bell of a blunder buss wobbling at him through a fissure in the wall.

"'Whom do you take me for?' says you, all innocent like," went on the voice sarcastically. "'The ruddy Customs,' says I, 'who goes spying round taverns and listening to the talk of poor drunkards in order to get on my track.' And what for? Why, for having given a hand with a tub or two to help the Dymchurch lads to a drink or two. We've had about enough of you ruddy Riding Officers, and I for one ain't standing much more."

"And I for another am not standing insult from any man, blunderbuss or no," replied Syn sharply. "You call me a Custom man, do you? Well, as a Marshman born and bred, I take that as an insult—a ruddy insult, as you seem to like that adjective. You, no doubt, are the Mister Mipps who works in Wraight's boatbuilding yard at Dymchurch-under-the-Wall. I know all about you from my friend Tony Cobtree, the Squire's son. You're a carpenter by trade and a smuggler for profit. I am no smuggler myself, perhaps for lack of opportunity, but my people, the Syns o' Lydd, have saved many a one from the gallows." A whistle of astonishment came from the other side of the wall, and the blunderbuss was withdrawn. "Ah, well, then, there's no quarrel, and I've been most damnably mistook in you, for which I asks your honour's pardon. A Syn o' Lydd, are you? Then you'll be old Mister Solomon's nephew, no doubt."

"Quite right. They call me Doctor Syn."

"What? A sawbones?"

"No, a parson. Come out of that fortification and shake hands."

"Not me, even though you ain't the ruddy Customs," replied the voice. "No showing myself on no skylines in case ruddy Customs does appear. Step in, and I'll give you as good a drink as ever you tasted. But I ain't coming out."

"I approve your caution, Mister Mipps," laughed the parson. "I'll come in, and if the drink you mention has not paid Customs it will of necessity taste the sweeter." So Doctor Syn, after tying his bridle to a ring in the wall, walked into the ruined bastion.

Mister Mipps gave the young parson the impression that had he not been born a man, he would have been bred a ferret, for the most striking feature in the little fellow was his nose—long, thin, and inquisitive-looking. As though to balance it, his hair, though scanty, was dragged back and twisted into a tarred queue which stuck out at the back. In addition, Mipps proved to be very thin, very small, dressed like a sailor, and carrying an atmosphere of important impertinence. And, again like a ferret, he was quick in movement and comically commanding.

"Glad to make you acquaintance, Mister Mipps," said the parson, holding out his hand.

Mipps wiped his on the skirt of his coat and welcomed his guest with a hard grip. He then removed the bung from a hand anker of brandy, a neat little cask bound with brass hoops. Doctor Syn drank with relish, and returned the anker.

Mipps in his turn drank deep.

"Good brandy never hurt nobody," he grinned.

"No, not even a parson," replied the Doctor with a smile.

"And I drinks to the Syns o' Lydd," said Mipps, handing the anker back again.

"And I drink to you," returned the Doctor, "and to all Marshmen, and may the Customs never get a one of them to hang upon the grisly tree of old Jack Ketch." Then, looking round the interior of the bastion, he added: "No wonder you preferred to shoot a Riding Officer rather than being carried away from here. It is all very cosy. I envy you this gypsy life. It is adventurous; it is simple and natural."

"Aye, sir," said Mipps, looking pleased. "A good clod fire always burning for food and warmth, and that there hurdle with broom on top for a shelter; what more can a man want?"

"Only brandy, it seems, and that you have," laughed Syn. "How long have you been in hiding here?"

"Couple of weeks," replied Mipps. "Though I'm thinking of moving myself on, and legging it down coast for Portsmouth."

"What do you want to go there for?" asked the parson.

"To ship for the West Indies," replied the little man. "Thinking of working my passage on a man o' war as ship's carpenter. Then I'll desert, 'cos they won't want for to lose me, being good at my work, and then I'll get down amongst the Brethren of the Coast."

"You mean go pirating?" asked Syn. "For that's all they are these days, I understand. The jolly buccaneers have given place to a scum of bloody-minded pirates. I suppose as a parson I should rebuke you for such a wish."

"Never rebuke a man for wishing to live a man's life and playing the man when he's in it," returned the other. "There's good and bad in every trade, and I expects piracy included. And I'll play the man with the dirtiest of 'em. Small I may be, but I've grit sharp as flint. A life of adventure for me. And from all accounts you gets it there. Battle, murder—"

"Aye, and sudden death," completed the Doctor.

"Aye, aye, sir," grinned Mipps; "but always allowing that you don't shoot first and straight."

"There's Execution Dock too," argued the parson. "Have you thought of that?"

"It's better to die in old England at the last," said Mipps. "Besides, some of us has been born with a rare talent for escape, and I'd never believe no one could hang me till I felt myself cut down."

"A true adventurer, I see," replied Doctor Syn; "and once more I envy you.

Whether you are boasting of your talents or not, I cannot say as yet, though it seems that they are to be put to an immediate test. While we have been talking I have had my eye on Lympne Castle, and it may interest you to know that three horsemen are riding down along the western wall. It is significant to me that they are heading in our direction, and that their leader is riding a dappled grey, very similar to mine."

"Sandgate swine," hissed Mipps, grasping his blunderbuss. "Well, I'll at least prove my boast about shooting first and straight."

"You'll attempt no such folly," retorted Syn sharply. "Unless of course you wish to forgo all possibility of becoming a good and bloody-minded pirate. You leave the officers to me, and you may yet see your battle and murder on the Spanish Main. Hold these, and keep yourself most religiously out of sight." Doctor Syn had quickly unbuttoned his long black riding-coat, and from one of his breeches pockets had taken out a handful of coins. Then he counted into the little man's hand, saying: "Three guinea spades, two crowns and a new fourpenny. Keep them safely and yourself hidden, or you'll hang." Waiting a few moments till the approaching riders were behind a clump of trees, he slipped out of the bastion walls and untethered his horse. By the time the officers had emerged from the trees he was slowly climbing the hill towards them, and since there were many other ruins scattered about the hillside, there was nothing to connect with the bastion occupied by Mipps. Meanwhile, the fugitive, with his weapon at the ready, cautiously peeped through a hole in the wall, straining his ears to listen to whatever the parson might say. This was easy enough, since the voice of the officer turned out to be coarse, loud and overbearing, while that of the parson extremely clear-spoken.

The officer was the first to speak. "Have you seen anything, you, sir, of a dirty-looking little rat of a man in this immediate neighbourhood?"

"I was about to put the very same question to you, sir," replied Doctor Syn; "for he must have passed within a few yards of you as he went up the hill but now. I hope for your own sakes that you are not as anxious as I am to lay him by the heels."

"Considering he's an approved smuggler and we are Riding Officers for Customs," replied the officer, "I should say that no one could be more anxious than we are to shackle him. What's your quarrel with the rascal?"

"Just this," replied Syn, making a wry face as he turned out the empty lining of his breeches pocket. "He came upon me unawares, and relieved this very pocket of three guinea-pieces, two crowns, and a silver fourpenny."

"And you offered no resistance?" asked the officer scornfully. "An agile man like you, tall, young and commanding, should have been a match for that little rat. Or did you resist him and let him get the better of you?" Doctor Syn shook his head. "I did not resist for two reasons. First, I am a parson and man of peace. And secondly I preferred to give him my gold rather than let him give me his lead."

"Aye, and the reverend young gentleman's quite right," said one of the other officers. "That there Mipps would pull a blunderbuss at a man as soon as I would at a rabbit."

"Which way did he go? Up the hill, you said? And it's just time for the carrier's cart to start for Ashford. He'll no doubt use some of your money to save his legs. Come on, my lads, we'll ride him down yet," And the officer turned his horse.

"I'll be vastly obliged if you catch him," called out the parson. "I am but now on my way to lodge complaint with Sir Henry Pembury, who is a Justice of the Peace. I am Doctor Syn, residing at the Court-House of Dymchurch, and I shall be grateful if you can return at least some of the money to that house. Sir Charles Cobtree is also a magistrate, as you may know."

"We'll catch the bit of gallows meat before he gets much farther, don't you worry," and, followed by his assistants, the officer set his spurs to his horse and galloped up the hill.

When it was safe for Doctor Syn to return to the bastion, he found his comical little companion chuckling. "Well, you certainly settled them very neat, sir. But I must first give you the lie and return the money. Here it is."

"No indeed," smiled the parson. "So long as you have it I have told no lie except that you went up the hill. Instead, I strongly advise you to go down it.

Get on to the friendly Marsh, and use the money to help you the quicker towards Portsmouth. Were it not for my cloth and duty, I should be tempted to accompany you. Together we could rule it royally amongst the pirates. Who knows but that we might not terrorize the Spanish Main?"

"Well, sir," replied Mipps with a wink, "if ever you should tire of your pulpit, go a-voyaging and fall into my hands, I pledge you my solemn word that I will not make you walk the plank. You shall walk the poop-deck with a sword at your side and a sash stuffed with pistols. Success to us both. Long life for the King, and Down with the Government and Customs." Doctor Syn laughed, and humorously drank the proffered toast, adding that should he ever tire of his own profession in England, he would leave his beloved brethren to another's cure and seek out the wilder Brethren of the Coast, where no doubt he and Mister Mipps might forgather on the poop of some black pirate ship.

Great would have been the astonishment of these ill-assorted companions had they realized that very soon their joking was to turn into grim reality.

Ignorant of this, however, they parted after mutual commendations of Good Luck, Mipps shouldering his few bundled possessions and taking the lower road for Portsmouth, by way of Dymchurch and Rye, and Doctor Syn leading his horse up the steep incline to Lympne Castle.

At the top of the hill, under shadow of the old bulwarks, he turned and looked back upon the flat Marshland, intersected with the silvery ribboned water of the dykes, and spread out beneath him like a vast map. He was amused to see that his little companion had already reached the dyke, and from somewhere in the grass Mipps had discovered a long plank, which he had successfully pushed across the water, and over this perilous bridge the little man was now walking. And then there came, owing to his former conversation with Mister Mipps, the first line of a chanty that was destined to become the terror of the pirate crews. "Oh, here's to the feet that have walked the plank".

Aye, aye, sir, a grim slogan that was to strike fear into the very fo'c'sles of the worst ships flying the Jolly Roger. Mister Mipps wobbled over to the other side of the dyke and then turned round and waved. Doctor Syn waved back.

Chapter 2. Doctor Syn Becomes a Squire of Dames

Sir Henry Pembury received his young clerical visitor in the Great Hall of the Castle. He apologized for not rising to greet him by pointing to his right foot, which, heavily bandaged, rested upon a stool in front of the large armchair in which he sat.

"I must ask your pardon also for having put you to the trouble of climbing Lympne Hill, but, you see, Doctor Syn, since this mountain of gout could not go to Mahomet, I had to ask you to come to me instead. Also the nature of the request I have to put to you makes it more convenient for you to be here, so that you may see with your own eyes what you are letting yourself in for. But first may I ask you when you think of journeying back to Oxford?"

"A week today, sir," replied Doctor Syn.

"And how did you propose to get there?" went on Sir Henry. "By the stagecoach or private conveyance?"

"By neither, sir," returned the Doctor. "I ride there on horseback, and I am glad to say that my good friend Tony Cobtree is to ride with me."

"But I understand from Sir Charles that his son had finished with the University."

"So he has, sir. More than a year since. He is revisiting the town on a more romantic mission than book-learning. He is taking a proposal of marriage to the lady of his affections."

"That's capital!" cried the Squire of Lympne heartily, as, without thinking, he brought his had crashing down on to his bad leg. That caused him such excruciating pain that it was some time before he could continue speaking.

In the meantime Doctor Syn expressed his sympathy by saying that he was surprised that so young a man as Sir Henry should be plagued with an old man's disease.

"Aye," replied the other, as he slowly recovered. "I'm still just on the right side of fifty, but I'm running to fat, and refuse to give up my two bottles of port for the whole faculty of doctors. My tailor could as easily persuade me to wear an ill-fitting coat. But to return to this Oxford business. You may or may not be aware that I undertook recently a Government mission to Spain. While in Madrid, my wife and I were lavishly entertained by a wealthy South American family. We naturally extended to them the hospitality of

Lympne Castle if by any lucky chance they visited England. It has proved, however, a most unlucky chance that has brought them here. The father died suddenly, and the mother and daughter are now travelling to deaden their grief. In short, they have been with us here for the last fortnight. Lady Pembury is very attached to them both, and wished them to stay indefinitely, but it so happens that they have to transact some business with a gentleman of Oxford concerning a mutual property in Spain, and since the roads are none too safe for foreign ladies travelling alone, I wonder now whether you and young Cobtree will undertake to be Squires of Dames and ride as their escort, since you are also bound for Oxford?"

"For myself, sir, it will be an honour," replied Doctor Syn, "and I know I can say the same for Tony." Sir Henry leaned forward and whispered. "You will not regret it. The widow is beautiful, but the daughter is ravishing. The mere fact that young Cobtree has already given his heart to a girl in Oxford will give you a clear field with the young beauty." Doctor Syn smiled. "I had no idea you were a matchmaker, sir." Sir Henry winked. "You wait till you see her, my lad," he laughed. But then his face went grave and he shook his head. "Ah, no, of course not. I had forgotten your cloth."

"There is nothing against a parson marrying, sir," said Syn.

"Like enough," returned the other, "but everything against an English parson wedding a Spanish Catholic, I should say."

"Well, that question need hardly trouble us, sir," smiled the Doctor, "for I have not yet seen the lady, much less fallen in love with her, and even though I did, 'tis ten to one that the lady might not fall in love with me."

"I think there is no need for you to mortify yourself," said the Squire. "You seem to me to be a young gentleman who will always get what he wants in this world."

"I hope you are a true prophet, upon my soul, sir," replied Syn. As he looked up the door opened and she was standing there, like a fresh painting set in the old oak panelling. The young scholar gasped in wonder, and slowly rose to his feet. He knew that he was gazing at what he wanted more than all the world.

She was dressed simply in the black mourning for her father, with a priceless mantilla crowned high and falling in cascades of lacy folds. The only colour a red rose caught into the meshes of her black hair. The elegant aloofness of the young scholar in his black riding dress had arrested her in the same bewildered astonishment. They forgot the presence of Sir Henry, who, secretly amused, was the first to break the spell.

"Se—orita," he called, "let me present to you my good young friend Christopher Syn, a learned Doctor of Oxford. Doctor Syn, this is Miss Imogene Almago, of whom we were but now talking." The Doctor was the first to move. He crossed the room with long, easy strides. The girl watched his approach, and smiled when he bent over her hand and raised it gently to his lips.

"I should add to my introduction," went on Sir Henry, "that this gentleman is to be your escort when you leave our county for Oxfordshire."

"I am greatly honoured," said Doctor Syn in a voice that was low, yet clear and caressing.

"Bring the se—orita to a chair over here," said Sir Henry. "And I shall delight in seeing you two the better acquainted."

Then Doctor Syn heard Imogene speak for the first time, in a voice mellow with the richness of the South. Her English was perhaps slow and a trifle stilted, but King's English for all that.

"I was sent by Her Ladyship to ask of you, Sir Henry, whether there was aught you needed before we take our usual walk round the improvements on the Castle grounds. They await me with the flower baskets upon the terrace, where the peacocks walk."

"Then take Doctor Syn with you, child, and become the better acquainted yourselves, or with Lady Pembury's help," replied Sir Henry. "But is there aught you can do for me, you say? Aye, there is. Two requests to one man.

Summon that rascally old butler of mine and tell him that Sir Henry would take the physic ordered him by the Doctor Sennacherib Pepper. It is, tell him, a full flagon of sherry sack, and in it, my dear young friends, I shall drink to your good healths. I am sure, too, Se—orita, that you will remember enough of our English to inform him that Doctor Syn, your escort here, is consenting to stay with us for dinner." Doctor Syn bowed his thanks to the Squire of Lympne, saying, "I am neither impertinent enough nor so stupid as to disobey your orders, sir." Then, turning to the girl and offering her his arm, added, "May I help you, Se—orita, to find the butler and deliver Sir Henry's commands?" The young Doctor, knowing the Castle well, escorted his beautiful charge on air to the pantries, where he delivered the Squire's messages. He then took pains to take a roundabout way to the terrace, finding, to his great relief, that Lady Pembury and the Spanish widow had left it solitary but for the peacocks.

Imogene, who, owing to her father's death and the

strangeness of a foreign land, had been considered reserved and shy, found herself talking more freely than she had thought possible to this young scholar. And Doctor Syn, who had been so often rallied by his friend Tony for not attempting a success amongst the ladies, realized that in this young girl was a cure for all his shyness and aloofness. He knew also that in her companionship he could be more than compensated for the loss of parents and relatives that had forced his young life into a loneliness that was unnatural.

Now, like all good Marshmen, Doctor Syn had been bred to understand their natural enemy, the sea: the sea which angrily waited to destroy the great seawall which kept their pastures safe. He was a fine swimmer, and knew something of sail, of tides and winds. But he confessed afterwards to Tony Cobtree that he had never been so proud of his skill in navigation as he was that morning in successfully avoiding a meeting in the wide grounds of Lympne with Lady Pembury and the girl's mother. No sooner did he descry them in the distance than he tacked away on another course which kept himself and his consort on an uninterrupted steering. Therefore, by the time he exchanged greetings with the elder ladies on their return to the Castle, the two young people had learned a good deal about each other.

Having spent many happy years at the University, and knowing the best families in the district, Doctor Syn was naturally interested to know what house they were visiting in Oxford. The daughter, who spoke English more fluently than her mother, explained that they were bound to Iffley, on the outskirts of the town, and were to reside there with the Squire until such time as certain business connected with her father's will could be settled. The Squire's nephew, on Nicholas Tappitt, had secured an important position under the British Ambassador at Madrid. Through some unfair treatment, as the girl pointed out sympathetically, the young man had lost his post, and having a liking for Spain as well as for the sea, he had enlisted the influence of Se—or Almago, who provided him with a ship in which to carry his own fruit-produce to England and the Netherlands. In this way Nicholas, for whom they seemed to have a liking, was able to remain in Spain in spite of his lost position. "My dear father believed in Nicholas," said the girl. "And whatever the trouble may have been at the Embassy, we were all convinced that Nicholas was not to blame." Doctor Syn, knowing something of the said Nicholas, thought otherwise, for this plausible young rascal had been sent down from his college owing to an unsavoury scandal connected with a serving-wench. He kept his opinion, though allowing himself to consider Imogene's fine sympathy wasted on such a rapscallion.

Hearing that Doctor Syn was acquainted with Squire Tappitt, the Spanish ladies pressed him for information concerning him and the Iffley estate. Here the young Doctor found himself in an awkward dilemma, for certainly what he knew of the uncle was a good deal more unpalatable than his knowledge of the nephew, for, known as Bully Tappitt, the Iffley Squire was shunned by all God-fearing people in the neighbourhood. Coarse, and brutally strong, with the worst reputation where women were concerned, he was the last man Doctor Syn would have wished to play the host towards his new-found friend and already adored Imogene. So he answered all their questions concerning Iffley and the Squire as evasively as possible, inwardly rejoicing that he was to be their escort, and determined that they should transact any necessary business with the Squire of Iffley from some quiet lodgings in the town, where he and Tony could keep protective watch.

During dinner, set out on a round table, where Doctor Syn sat between Lady Pembury and the Spanish girl, the latter talked so much about Nicholas that the young cleric for the first time in his life suffered the worst pangs of jealousy.

She afforded him the acutest agony as she recounted the many churches, parties and theatres to which the rascal has escorted her. She told him how very fond she was of him, how vastly he amused her with his funny ways, how much she admired his adventurous spirit in becoming a businessman after his forced failure as a diplomat.

"But I loved him best," she said—"oh yes, very much indeed—when he told me he was desperately in love with me, but even better still when he most solemnly asked me to marry him." With his spirits at the lowest ebb, Doctor Syn managed to ask her, "And what did you answer?"

"I?" she whispered. "Why, I laughed in his face. I told him that my very life would be in danger from all the other women he had put the same question to that very day. And it is true. He has a way with him. But oh, too reckless! They say that when he goes up to woo a lady in her drawing-room, he will make proposals to the serving-maid upon the stairs. He is a rake, my dear sir."

"I admit he was when I knew him," returned Syn. "And so neither of you took the proposal very seriously, I take it?" he added, with his heart much lighter.

"He did," she laughed. "At one time he was so serious in he protestations that he ran out of our house to the nearest church, embraced the Catholic Faith, and was surprised that such devotion did not sway me. But how could I marry a man who would forget the fact whenever he saw another petticoat in view?"

"Also you would not think of marrying a fool," whispered Doctor Syn. "And the man who, having once seen you, could think of another woman would prove himself the worst of fools, in my thinking."

"That is very kindly put," she answered. "But, do you know, I think that you are even quicker than poor Nicholas in saying the pretty thing."

"But I have never said a pretty thing to a lady before in all my life," he replied. "And except to you, I never shall. From the first moment I saw you in the doorway, I knew well that I loved you. I do love you, and for me there will be no other woman."

"Then may I ask you a favour—a great favour?" she whispered.

"I will do anything for you," he whispered back. "What is it?"

"That you will tell me that again when we are alone beneath the stars? Will you?"

"When? Soon?"

"I hope so," she breathed back gently.

Now, it was easier than might be imagined for these two young lovers to whisper about such intimate things. First the girl's mother, who sat directly opposite, was slow to understand English, and both her host and hostess had moved their chairs as close to hers as possible, so that they could speak the plainer in her ears. Also Sir Henry, who was secretly enjoying this ripening love affair, tactfully moved a large bowl of flowers, which screened their faces into a comparative privacy, and of this Doctor Syn certainly made the best advantage, for just before Lady Pembury suggested that they should retire to the drawing-room and leave the gentlemen to their port, he had taken Imogene's hand in his beneath the table, had felt an answering pressure to his own, and then seen, to his utmost joy, her lips frame silently the words, "I love you too." Then, owing to Sir Henry's gout, he claimed the privilege of escorting the ladies to the door, and since the girl was last to leave, he managed to whisper without the butler hearing, "Upon the terrace. Soon. Beneath the stars." And the look she gave him was assent.

All very romantic, and cleverly done. But Doctor Syn had really no cause to think, as he did, that he had deceived not only

Sir Henry, but the butler; for as he gazed after the girl until she disappeared into the drawing-room, Sir Henry was guilty of bestowing a solemn wink upon the ancient and stately manservant, who respectfully and solemnly returned the wink to his master. But of this Doctor Syn was ignorant, as he returned to the table and, picking up his glass, toasted "All beneath the roof of Lympne Castle."

"Sit down here, Doctor," said the Squire of Lympne. "I told you that you seemed to be the sort of young man who can get what he wants, and I am most eager to help you."

"That is very good of you, sir," replied Doctor Syn, with a smile of gratitude.

"I suggest," continued Sir Henry, "that I despatch one of my stable-men down to Dymchurch with a note from me to say that you are staying the night with us here, for it has occurred to me that the evenings being still long, the stars may be plaguey late coming out upon the terrace."

"Faith, sir," laughed the Doctor, "either I talk too loud, or your hearing is very acute."

"Or your speaking is always clear, even in your whisperings," said Sir Henry. "But listen to my further suggestions, and see if they commend themselves to you. Tomorrow you will escort the lady and her Spanish companions to Dymchurch, and make them acquainted with our good friends, the Cobtrees. Sir Charles, being your guardian, will no doubt be glad of the opportunity of looking well upon the face and person of the Se—orita, for I may drop such a hint to him in my letter. I then suggest that while he talks with our Spanish ladies, you take the opportunity of packing up your traps and having them put into the boot of my coach. I then suggest that you persuade the Cobtrees how very essential it is for you to return to Lympne and finish your vacation with us. Young Cobtree will certainly excuse you, since he must be in the same frame of mind which your visit to Lympne has framed you in too. My further suggestion is that, since the Se—orita is a keen horsewoman, and owing to the fact that your whisperings inside the coach might be too clear, you two shall ride behind the coach at a distance sufficient to avoid the dust of the wheels. I mention the back of the coach in order that my good coachman shall have nothing to distract his attention from the horses before him. And now, if you are in agreement, bring me those writing materials, and I will pen the letter on the table here. But let me first recharge our glasses, and drink to Doctor Syn, and one other that shall be nameless."

"And to our kind host," replied the Doctor.

"And since I like to be undisturbed when toiling with the pen," went on Sir Henry, "I suggest that when you have helped me finish this bottle, you rejoin the ladies in the drawing-room." Before carrying out this last suggestion, Doctor Syn unfolded his anxiety concerning the Squire of Iffley, telling Sir Henry in confidence all that he knew of the uncle and the nephew.

To this, Sir Henry listened gravely, and then asked, "How long is it since you visited these Tappitt people, then?"

"For nearly a year I have avoided Iffley," replied Syn. "I formed the opinion they were not the sort of people with whom a clerical official of my college should be associated. I have too many young and impressionable youths under my charge, and have to set them an example. Warning them against such rakes as the Tappitts, I had in all honesty to take the warning to myself."

"And have you heard nothing of the uncle since?" asked Sir Henry.

"Nothing to his credit, believe me, sir."

"You tell me that he had a bad reputation where women were concerned," went on Sir Henry. "But when you knew him, he was a bachelor, I understand."

"He certainly had no wife to insult with the presence of the many questionable ladies that resorted there."

"Then, since a woman can so often change a man for the better," said Sir Henry, "perhaps even Bully Tappitt has mended his ways. I have a letter here that you may read. The Se—ora had another couched in the same terms. As you see, this is addressed to Lady Pembury and myself, telling us what a pleasure it will be to receive our Spanish guests, and asking when they may expect them. It is signed, as you see, by Elinor Tappitt, wife to the Squire of Iffley." Saying which, he handed the parson a letter which he took from his pocket.

Doctor Syn read the letter through, and then glanced up at Sir Henry. "Well, sir," he said, "at the risk of seeming suspicious and perhaps uncharitable, I believe this letter to be false.

"The Squire of Iffley thinks, quite rightly, that if our Spanish ladies realize he is a bachelor and has no wife to welcome and protect them, they would decline to sojourn under his roof. This would not suit Bully Tappitt. He needs money for his gaming, and if he can get our friends into his power he will do what he likes with their money. Now, I know a landlady in Oxford of the strictest integrity, where our friends could be lodged most comfortably, and I suggest, sir, in my turn, that we shall be fortunate in having Tony Cobtree in our company, for since he has already been called to the Bar, his advice on any document that may be presented to the ladies for signature will be of the greatest help."

"And the very nature of his journey will keep him in Oxford some time, no doubt," laughed Sir Henry. "Well, my lad, since you are to be the ladies' escort, you must be allowed your own discretion in regard to their welfare, and should this Squire of Iffley be contemplating any rascally tricks, I warrant you and young Cobtree will be more than a match for him."

"I hope we may be, sir," replied Doctor Syn. "For my part, I shall depart from the usual custom of my cloth and buckle on my father's sword."

"But however brave your steel," cautioned Sir Henry, "see that it is tempered with good caution, for to make enmity with a noted duellist is no light undertaking."

"At the worst, sir, I should not be unprepared," replied the Doctor, "for since taking orders I have never given up the practice of many accomplishments. In riding, fence and marksmanship I have been in continual training, and with right upon my side and a reasonable amount of luck, backed by mine own skill, I have yet to meet the man whom in a righteous quarrel I should avoid."

"And since Christ says in Holy Writ that He brought a sword to the Earth, I fail to see why His own parsons should be scorned to be skilled in 'em," said the Squire of Lympne solemnly.

After which understanding between these two gentlemen, Doctor Syn went to join the ladies.

And long after the Squire of Lympne had despatched his rider with the letter for Sir Charles Cobtree upon Romney Marsh, the early night stars played their romantic parts upon the terrace of the Castle, so that when at last good-nights were said in the corridors of Lympne, Doctor Syn was confident that his authority with the Spanish ladies went a little further than mere escort, for Imogene gave him cause to believe that their families were almost united.

Certain it was that Doctor Syn desired no better.

The next day the faithful coachman to Sir Henry reported to his master that the expedition to Dymchurch-under-the-Wall was a great success. His "Everything-seems-very-promising-your-Honour" was optimistic news to Sir Henry, and it did the coachman no harm in reporting it, for Sir Henry, despite his gout, was still

romantically inclined, and happened to be fond of both his young
Spanish guest and the brilliant nephew of his own attorney
Solomon Syn.

Imogene loved Dymchurch, and all the good folk she met
there. Sir Charles Cobtree went out of his way to make the place
seem attractive to her.

"Persuade young Christopher to marry, my dear, and then tell
him to leave Oxford and retire here as our Vicar. The people need
a married parson here.

Our present incumbent wishes to retire. Well, he is old, I'll
admit. But I've badgered the old fellow to stay on till my good
young friend is ready to take his place. Let him bring Dymchurch
a Vicar's wife, and the living's his."

"I love it all, my Christopher," she whispered on the ride back
to Lympne beneath the stars. "But oh, my dear, your little
churches, and your great ones too, of the Protestant Faith are so
very plain and dull compared with the glories of ours. But I love
you, dear. Yes, I put you before religion."

"But could you change your faith for mine?" asked the parson.

"Oh, but I could do more for you than ever the stupid poor
dear headstrong Nicholas did for me," she answered. "If he could
change his faith for mine because of love, cannot my love make me
change mine too, because I happen so to think of you? My church
is now you, and my faith and ritual is my love for you. Do you love
me as well?"

"I think I would give up all for you," he answered. "But you
could never ask me to give up faith and honour. You also could
never give up honour, and I do not ask you to give up your own
country's faith."

"But I shall, and of my own free will; and yes, because of you.
But you must still allow me to think that the churches of the
Protestants are, oh, so dull!"

"Your presence in them will make them the more lively," he
smiled back.

But that speech of hers he was destined to remember through
a twenty years' Odyssey of bitterness.

However, there was no thought of bitterness during that
blessed week, so skillfully prepared by the Squire of Lympne, and
certainly no bitterness in that long ride beside the coach to Oxford.
A face at the coach window. A beloved rider outside. A loyal
companion in the handsome Tony Cobtree, who lingered for his
friend's sake, although so impatient to reach their goal for his own

ends.

A long, romantic journey, and no mishap to mar it. But everything to make it wonderful. Romance and Love. Until at last Doctor Syn rides out to Iffley to inform the Squire that his betrothed, one Imogene Almago, and her mother are awaiting to receive him in their lodgings at Oxford, and that their attorney will be there at his convenience any morning to discuss business.

Chapter 3. Doctor Syn Escapes

The large mansion at Iffley stood in its own distinctive grounds, and was hidden by trees. A high wall ran round three sides, and the river completed the circle of defence upon the fourth.

Doctor Syn rode to the Lodge gates, and without dismounting rang the bell.

A forbidding-looking man-servant came out from the Lodge and asked him his business. He opened one side of the great gates with an ill grace, and Doctor Syn noted that he locked it again directly he had passed through.

Now, it so happened that the Squire of Iffley had heard that Doctor Syn had forbidden his pupils to play cards or dice, and as this had been one of the Bully's sources of income, he was enraged to see the cause of his disappointment riding up the drive.

Bully Tappitt did not wait for his servant to open the front door. He opened it himself, and, grabbing a heavy whip from a handy peg, strode out in a fine rage on to the porch steps.

"And what the devil brings you here?" he asked brusquely. "I thought you had warned your companions against visiting me. However, if you are here to play behind their backs, I am your man, with cards or dice in secret."

"I am not here for gaming, sir," replied Doctor Syn, without dismounting. "I bring you a message from a lady."

"The devil you do," laughed the Squire. "Come in your official position as a parson, no doubt. Well, understand that I am not paying compensation to any woman who has had the privilege of my attentions."

"There is no question of attentions in this case, sir," replied Doctor Syn coldly. "You have not had the honour of meeting the lady in question, and she will only extend you that honour in the presence of myself and her English legal adviser, Mr. Antony Cobtree. She will receive you at White Friars House, St.

Giles', tomorrow at noon, if you desire to interview her concerning your nephew's affairs in Spain."

"Are you talking of the Almago women from Madrid?" asked Tappitt.

"I have the honour to be speaking on behalf of the Se—ora

Almago, sir."

"Are they in Oxford, then?" he demanded.

"They are, sir," went on Syn. "I myself have lodged them with the good woman who lets the apartments I named."

"But they were to come here. What the devil!" exploded the Squire. "Why are they not here? I invited them."

"Pardon me, sir. The invitation was null and void, and under the circumstances demanded no reply." Doctor Syn spoke quietly, but with a cold disdain. "The letter did not come from you. It came, in fact, from nobody, for, as I pointed out to my good friends at Lympne Castle, and have since confirmed it, there is no such person as Elinor Tappitt, wife to the Squire of Iffley. You are a bachelor."

"And who are you to interfere with my schemes—" started the Squire.

"Schemes, eh?" repeated the Doctor. "I can well believe that. I will tell you my authority. I am the prospective son-in-law to the Se—ora. Yes, sir, her daughter, the Se—orita, with her mother's consent, has promised to marry me."

"Marry you?" retorted the Squire. "We'll see about that. I rather think she will marry my nephew."

Doctor Syn shook his head. "She has already refused him, sir."

"Then if he's such a fool as I always suspected, she shall marry me," said the Squire. "Or I'll marry the widow, and then refuse you the daughter. Yes, sir, I'll brook no interference from a hypocritical young parson, who no doubt thinks to get the dead Spaniard's money into his own coffers."

"There is no more to be said, I think, sir. Tomorrow at noon. Good day."

"Oh no," replied the Squire. "Not good day yet. I have not finished with you."

"But I have with you till noon tomorrow," replied Doctor Syn, turning his horse's head down the long drive and riding slowly away.

"I think not, till my grooms have done with you," cried the Squire. He then bawled out the words: "Stables, quick! All of you!" Doctor Syn saw him run into the stable yard, and so put his own horse to the canter.

The drive was a long one through an avenue of trees. Fortunately the young parson knew the lie of the ground. He remembered that there was a back lane from the stables which was a short cut to the Lodge gates. He remembered that these gates were locked. Even at the gallop he could hardly reach them and persuade the man to open before the arrival of the half-dozen bullies that Bully Tappitt kept to do other and dirtier work than grooming. Just as he was considering the possibility of attempting a gallop, he heard the deep bell clanging from the stable tower, and guessed that this must be a signal to the lodge-keeper to stop him. The bell was followed by a banging of doors, cries from stablemen, cracking of whips, and then the full-throated baying of hounds.

Doctor Syn had no intention of riding into such disadvantage. He knew well that Bully Tappitt would not scruple to go to extremes. This at the best would be a flogging, perhaps injury to his horse, and then as an excuse a trumped-up accusation of libellous interference, which the Squire would lodge against him to the College authorities. The odds were too heavy to risk. It was then that a richer way out occurred to him.

Turning his horse sharp to the right, he rode through the woods, along the mossy path that led to the river. The Isis ran there broad and wide, but it would not be the first time that the young scholar had swum his horse, and he considered that a wetting and a laugh against Tappitt in the face of his bullies were preferable to a bad manhandling. He was no coward, as he was to show by the different risk he was to take, but as a lover he was not desirous to court any facial disfigurement.

So he galloped through the wood in the opposite direction taken by his would-be assailants. Just as he approached the boathouse, a voice cried out, "Now, then, sir, what do you want?" A heavily built waterman barred his way. He was armed with a short, sharp boat-hook.

The Doctor reined in his horse. "I have been talking to your master, the Squire of Iffley," he answered pleasantly, waving his hand towards the river.

"He thinks that this little ditch is unswimmable, on horseback. You know how given he is to a wager. I am about to prove to him that a good horse and rider find it easy. What do you think?"

"I think not," growled the boatman. "The stable bell has been clanging, and that means 'close all ways out of the estate'."

"If you come here, I'll give you good reason not to detain me," replied Doctor Syn, affably putting his hand into his breeches pocket. He saw the covetous glint come into the other's eye. He read his thought, "If this fool cares to hand me a guinea to get out of here, I'll take it, stop him leaving and then deny his gift to my master." Doctor Syn sure enough held up the guinea invitingly with his right hand.

The man approached, and put out one hand for the coin, and with the other tried to grasp the rein. The rider shortened rein to prevent this, and at the same time distracted the other's attention with a sudden "Hallo! Is this a good one? I believe not. I've been done brown. I should have rung them one by one. It looks to me—well, dull."

"I'll ring it," said the other eagerly. "Let's see."

"I'll try it in my teeth," answered Syn.

He suited the action to the word; put the coin between his teeth, and made a face as though biting hard.

The man waited for his judgment, eyeing the guinea held so firmly in the young man's white teeth. Instead he should have kept his eye on the young man's right hand. The fist closed, and a terrific blow caught the waterman under the jaw. Down the bank he rolled into the water, and down the bank went horse and rider straight into the river; and by the time the man scrambled for the bank and held his jaw, Doctor Syn was in midstream heading for the bank.

The current was stronger than he thought, and swept his horse below the opposite landing-stage, but Doctor Syn headed for a meadow belonging to a little farm, intending to land there, despite a notice on a tree which said, "Trespassers will be prosecuted." The owner of the farm happened to be out with a fowling-piece under his arm, and, objecting to the swimming would-be trespasser, cried out: "Now then, if, as I saw, you come from yonder cursed place, you should know what to expect from me if you attempt to touch my bank. I've suffered enough from the sins of the Tappitt crowd, so my advice is, swim back as fast as you can, lest I drill holes in you."

"I've just escaped from there, my good friend," Doctor Syn called back. "I preferred a wetting to a whipping from the rascals. So of your charity let me land here, or my horse may drown."

"Who are you, then?" asked the farmer cautiously.

"A young doctor of Queen's College," he answered. "And with every cause to hate the folk behind me." The farmer immediately came down from the bank and pointed out the best spot for landing, which was no sooner accomplished than Doctor Syn was asking which was the best bridge to cross in order to come upon the road leading past the gates of Iffley Court, and on the way to Oxford.

"I wish to have the laugh of them from the safe side of their locked gates," he said. "Aye, and before they have discovered how I have tricked them, too," he added.

For this reason of haste, he refused the farmer's offer of a stable for his horse and grooming, while he should dry his clothes by the kitchen fire, and himself with a warming drink.

But for all his haste, the farmer insisted on rubbing down the horse with a wisp of grass, and as he did so he talked. "I'll show you the way beyond the house. You can gallop it in three minutes, while they'll be hunting you in the grounds, or waiting for you to break cover. You'll reach Iffley gates before that rogue you knocked into the Isis. I'll do anything against them over there. I have cause enough to hate them. Lend me your ear, for my wife is coming down the meadow, and what I would say is her grief." Thereupon he quickly whispered a foul story of seduction which the Squire of Iffley had carried out against their daughter. She had been taken across the river by boat, and sent back the next morning with money stitched into her clothing. At the end of this sad story the man chuckled grimly:

"But my revenge is coming, and little do they know how I am going to strike. I have planned with some cunning."

"It seems to me, then," said Doctor Syn, "that it were a good thing for the neighbourhood if this scoundrel should be removed to the place in which he rightly belongs."

"Aye, sir," replied the farmer. "And that is where I wish him, and I'll help him there too. The deepest Hell."

"The same place to which I was referring," nodded the parson dryly. "Well, keep your ears open for immediate gossip concerning him, and you may find that I have taken the responsibility of sending him there from your shoulders."

"Don't rob me of revenge. I live for it," pleaded the man. "Let me be some help to you."

"The time is not yet ripe. But soon I may ask your help," and with a wave of his hand and still dripping wet, Doctor Syn cantered out through the farmyard and galloped up the road to the bridge.

The farmer was right. He reached the gates in less than three minutes, but drew rein ere he came abreast of them, walking his horse along the grass footpath to avoid the noise.

But so much noise was the Squire of Iffley making with his curses and his riding-crop upon backs of hounds and stable-men that no one heard the rider approach or saw him peer through the gates with a grin. In the centre of the drive stood Tappitt, lashing out freely with his whip. Some half-dozen stablemen armed with cudgels and whips were staring up the drive.

"I tell you," cried the Squire, "that he can only get out this way. The coward is hiding in the trees somewhere. Loose those mastiffs and let 'em rout him out.

He can't get out of locked gates, or jump the wall."

"I'm afraid he has got out all the same," laughed Doctor Syn.

The Squire swung round with an oath, and stared at the rider through the gates.

"How the devil—" he began.

But Doctor Syn cut him short.

"I may be a parson, but I am also a good judge of horseflesh. I never ride a horse who cannot jump. But, my faith, the Isis is a broad ditch. However, a good horse is a good horse. Tomorrow? At noon? The attorney, the ladies and myself will await you at St. Giles'. Good day. I'm sorry I cannot stay longer to enjoy your sport and hospitality, but we tutors are hard-worked." And digging his heels in hard, Doctor Syn let his horse out into a full gallop towards Oxford.

Chapter 4. The Challenge

Just before noon on the following day Doctor Syn, Tony Cobtree, and the Spanish mother and daughter awaited the arrival of the Squire of Iffley.

White Friars, in which Doctor Syn had taken lodging for the ladies, was a pleasantly situated house with windows overlooking St. Giles' market. The Annual Fair was in full swing. Hundreds of merry-makers jostled each other good-humouredly to get to the various booths of entertainment and the gaily decorated stalls. From every street people were hurrying to swell the crowd.

With one arm encircling Imogene's waist, Doctor Syn leaned from the open window enjoying the scene.

"Our visitor from Iffley will be hard put to it in making his way through this lot," he laughed.

Antony Cobtree, who was seated at a table with the Se—ora, looked up from the legal papers he had been arranging.

"You seem very sanguine that he'll come," he answered. "For my part, I think he will not dare to show his face. The rascal has too many enemies amongst the townsfolk. When you made the appointment, you forgot the Fair, Christopher, and I am willing to lay you a guinea that he will not have the courage to swagger his way through that crowd."

"The bully is not without courage," replied Syn. "And I still think he will come."

"Are you willing, then, to lose your guinea?" asked the young lawyer.

"I rather fear you would lose yours," laughed the Doctor. "There's a coach just turning into the Market, and I can see the Iffley arms on the panel. The coachman seems to have as little regard for the crowd as his master has, for he's lashing out freely with his long whip, while our bully is poking his cane at them through the window. Come and see. There will be trouble, I think." Although the plunging horses had cleared a space with their hoofs, the crowd was so densely packed that those nearest to the coach could not press back out of reach from the lashings of the long whip, and the coachman standing up on his box fiercely struck at all within reach. Angry men were rushing the coach doors, but right and left the heavy knob of the Squire's long cane kept striking, and the oaths that followed each sickening thud proclaimed the fact that he had scored a hit.

"You idle dogs!" shouted the Squire. "Must I teach you to give way for your betters? If you want a lesson, I will give you one."

At this there was a growling protest from the crowd, and a woman's voice rang out with, "What happened to Betty Dale, the girl at Iffley Mill?"

"Aye, and a score of other poor lasses like Esther Sommers," cried another.

"And he dares drive his cattle into St. Giles'!" sang out a man.

The Squire flung open the door of the coach and shouted to the footman to get down and lead the near horse, which was still plunging. Leaving his cane in the coach, he then drew his sword and faced his assailants. They shrank back before the naked steel. They well knew his reputation, and feared the determined fury in his eyes. Conscious of his own power, he laughed and walked slowly to the horses' heads. The footman, who feared his master more than the angry crowd, climbed down from the high ledge at the back of the coach on which he stood, and followed the Squire to the front, where he grasped the bearing-reins and steadied the frightened animals.

"The times are bad indeed," said the Squire in a loud voice, "when a gentleman must needs cut a passage for his own coach through such scum.

Follow on my heels, you" (this over his shoulder to the terrified footman), "and we'll reach White Friars over dead bodies if any of these clodpoles oppose us." Thereupon he advanced so suddenly that those of the crowd immediately threatened by the Bully's weapon fell head over heels against their fellows behind them, who were so tightly packed before that they were seized with panic, and it was amidst groans from the fallen, shrieks from the women and children and curses from all, that the Squire of Iffley's equipage swept on towards White Friars.

Doctor Syn, still leaning from the parlour window which was on the first floor, saw that a lot of women and children were wedged in the crowd directly in front of the entrance to the house, so, leaving his companions, he ran down the white-panelled stairway, and, flinging open the front door, dragged those nearest into the safety of the hall, at the same time ordering others to follow their example. Thus a clearing was effected in front of the Squire's sword and the oncoming horses.

In this manner it did not take long to reach the house, where the Squire called a halt.

"Await me here," he cried to his servants, "and should any of this rabble annoy you further, do not scruple to use strong measures." He then addressed his stalwart coachman. "Get your artillery out of the boot, you fool, and if your whip don't do your business try flint-flashing." Whereupon the coachman stood up, put the whip in its socket, opened the locker beneath the box seat, and produced two horse-pistols and a blunderbuss, which he lay on the roof of the vehicle.

It was then that the Squire saw, to his further annoyance, that the way to the house was barred by the huddled women and children whom Doctor Syn was shepherding.

"Faith, must I cut my way through this lot, to keep an appointment?" At this, and the sight of his yet drawn sword, the children cried and whimpered, while some of the women set up a screaming. In a few moments, however, Doctor Syn managed to calm their fears, assuring them that he would see to their protection, and as soon as all was quiet he confronted the Squire, and spoke clearly enough for all to hear.

"I believe, sir, that you take great pride in your title of 'Bully'. It is an epithet after your own heart, and no doubt you consider 'Bully' Tappitt to be something of a fine fellow. In that I suggest you are wrong. If you look at a dictionary, providing, of course, that you can read—you will find that a bully is a coward. And the dictionary is right, sir, for what is more cowardly than a strong man oppressing those he thinks weaker than himself?" At this there was a murmur of approbation from the angry men who were grouped around the coach.

"Hold your tongues, you rascals, when you hear your betters speak." But more than his words, it was the sunlight gleaming on that naked blade that silenced them. At which the Squire, with a scornful laugh, turned his back on them and answered Doctor Syn.

"I think it takes more than a coward to have faced this mass of dangerous discontents alone, sir."

"I rather think that Bully Tappitt, in his vast conceit, saw no danger in it," replied the parson, with a sneer. "For your own safety, however, let me tell you that your situation is very dangerous; for, were I to use a little oratory against you, those stout fellows of Oxford Town would duck you in the horse-trough yonder. But I choose to do no such thing. My cloth forbids it. I am a man of peace. And I recommend these good people to ignore your brutalities, and to continue their merry-makings." At this some of the bolder spirits raised a cheer, but the Squire took no heed, but continued:

"Merry-makings?" he repeated. "This Fair is a scandal to the neighbourhood. What is it but an annual excuse for cheating, quarrelling, idle lewdness and drinking to excess?"

"Are you claiming a monopoly upon your own pet habits, sir?" asked the Doctor scornfully.

This the Squire ignored, as well as the laughter the remark caused amongst the crowd. He merely continued:

"I should have thought that the University, of which you are such a bright ornament, would have used what influence it has to stop this annual inconvenience."

"The University, sir, agrees with the God in Heaven Whom it tries to serve, in that the lives and happiness of these good people are vastly more important than the trifling inconvenience that may trouble gentlemen of your kidney." The Squire's sword twitched angrily, but on hearing a chorus of applause behind him, he had sufficient wisdom not to run his blade through the body of a defenceless man before the eyes of so many hostile witnesses.

"Have done with your incivilities, sir!" he cried angrily. "You take advantage of your cloth, and think yourself secure by toadying to peasants. I did not come here, at some inconvenience, to bandy words with you, but to transact a piece of business with some ladies. Lead the way."

"The sooner it's over the better," replied the Doctor.

He turned to lead the way, and saw that Tony Cobtree was standing in the porch. The young attorney was dressed in the height of fashion as became one of his station who had journeyed so far to woo his lady. The Squire saw him too, and noted that his fingers were playing a dangerous tattoo upon the beautifully chased gold hilt of his small-sword.

"Another security you had, eh, Doctor?" he sneered. "Your cloth and popularity amongst the commoners were not sufficient. You must have an armed coxcomb behind you."

"You would find but little of the coxcomb in either of us, sir, if it came to sword-play," replied Syn haughtily. "But we are not sufficiently interested to indulge you. Perhaps we set as much store upon the rules of duelling as you do, and just as you value your station in life—such as it is—why, so do we; and no man of breeding is considered dishonoured by declining to meet one whom he knows to be beneath him."

"Have done with your glib talk, Mister Parson!" rapped out the

Squire, "and let us transact our business with these foreign women. Where are they? And where is this Kentish lawyer that you spoke about?"

"Let me introduce myself, sir," retorted young Cobtree, coming forward.

"You, I understand, are this Iffley Squire, of whom we have heard small good. I am Antony Cobtree, Attorney at Law, and here for the convenience and protection of two respected Spanish ladies. I have been recommended for this office by my friend here, Doctor Syn of this University, and by two very distinguished Justices of the Peace in the County of Kent, one of them being Sir Henry Pembury of Lympne Castle, and the other my own father and his friend, Sir Charles Cobtree, Leveller of the Marsh Scotts of Romney, in the CourtHouse of Dymchurch-under-the-Wall. Let me add that my recommendation has been approved by the two honoured ladies who await you above. And let me add again that they are only willing to receive you as representing your ward and nephew, Mister Nicholas Tappitt, now absent in Spain, who was involved in generous business ties with the late Se—or Almago. These ladies now await you: the widow and the daughter of the said Spanish gentleman. Doctor Syn and myself are both busy men; and so if you will follow us to the parlour above, you shall hear the instructions regarding your ward." Saying which, young Cobtree led the way through the crowd of women and children in the hall.

Now, on the mention of the parlour above, the Squire of Iffley lifted his quizzing-glass and, surveying the window indicated, beheld the beautiful Imogene anxiously peering over the ledge.

The Squire, seeming not to have listened to the purport of the lawyer's speech, called upon Doctor Syn to wait.

"Is that young filly above there the wench whom my nephew has let slip through his purse-strings?"

Doctor Syn did not reply, but with an angry gesture pointed to the porch.

The Squire, however, did not immediately obey the invitation to enter the house. He continued to gaze at the Spanish girl, who, feeling the embarrassment, retired from the open window.

"I have always thought my nephew a fool," continued the Squire. "I am now so sure of it that if I do not marry the girl myself I shall at least cut him out of my testament. She is as beautiful as she is rich, and shall such a morsel be thrown away upon such a rapacious young parson as yourself? We'll soon see to that, sir. Lead me to this charmer, at once." Doctor Syn, who had kindly set the children aside to make a passage-way, now turned with an expression of suppressed fury upon the Squire of Iffley.

"You must please understand, sir," he said coldly, "that you are only permitted to enter here as a legal representative of your nephew. In short, to be quite frank, I do not intend to introduce you to my betrothed, so you will look upon this as merely a business interview. Follow me." Saying which, Doctor Syn followed young Cobtree into the hall.

Young Cobtree, who had overheard all and had reached the parlour first, instructed the ladies that it would not be seemly for either of them to rise, to curtsey, or in any way greet the scoundrel who unfortunately had to be admitted to the conference merely as the guardian of his nephew, and thus it was that when Doctor Syn said, "This is the Squire of Iffley, and uncle to your acquaintance Nicholas Tappitt, who is here at the request of your legal representative," neither of the ladies so much as bowed an acknowledgment to the Squire's elaborate bow in the doorway. Realizing that he was ignored, however, did not prevent him from raising his quizzing-glass and surveying with audible sighs the young Imogene.

"I think we will close the windows," said young Cobtree. "I shall never be able to make myself clear to you, sir, with all this noise. In point of fact, sir, the crowd is grown so hostile against you that on the completion of our interview I think you will be hard put to it to reach your home at Iffley with a whole skin.

Kindly sit down there." And he pointed to an empty chair at the table.

This the Squire surveyed through his quizzing-glass as he approached it, pretended to perceive dust upon the seat, which he flicked away with a large handkerchief, and continued the insulting gesture till young Cobtree had closed the window.

"If the chair is not to your liking, sir," he said, as he sat down in front of his papers, "I am sure the ladies will allow you to stand. It will at least lend you a show of respect."

The Squire placed one hand idly on the back of the chair, and raising his glance once more, surveyed the elder lady quickly, passed on to the younger, and surveyed her longer, while uttering a sigh of longingness.

"Although these gentlemen," he said, waving his hand towards Doctor Syn and young Cobtree, "seem as desirous as their friends without to place me at a disadvantage with you, I assure you both, dear ladies, that I am ravished to meet such beauty, and would wish nothing better than to be your very humble servant." An elaborate bow before continuing: "I extend to you a very hearty welcome to England and to Oxford. Perhaps I owe you an apology. Doctor Syn has already corrected me for the letter of invitation I sent to you at Lympne Castle. It was supposed to come from my wife. You will ask me why I acted this lie. My excuse is that I was anxious to play the humble host to you, and am still anxious to do so. Not being versed in the conventions of Spain, I feared that, did you know I was a bachelor, you might feel inclined to refuse my hospitality. Let me assure you that in England the presence of my lady housekeeper ensures that all proper conventions would be observed. Also when I wrote I was ignorant that this very fortunate young parson had been more successful than my nephew in having won the heart of this lady. Had I known of this, I should have extended my hospitality to him. This I still do. Doctor Syn, you are welcome at Iffley for as long as these ladies will honour me with their presence." Doctor Syn was about to reply, but Imogene interrupted him with a gesture.

"My mother speaks but little English, sir," she said, addressing the Squire, "so no doubt you will allow me as her medium. My mother has come to England to seek quiet after her bereavement. We are very comfortable here in these rooms found for us by Doctor Syn. She would not feel happy if we were to thrust ourselves upon you as guests, lest our own sadness communicate itself to others of your household."

"Bless you, my dear young lady," laughed the Squire, "you may both of you cry all day, if you be in the mind, and I'll give orders that all at Iffley shall cry with your for company and to put you at your ease."

"I think, sir," put in Doctor Syn, "that we can let any question of your hospitality alone. Since I have forbidden my own students to visit you, I shall advise these ladies in the same manner. Mr. Cobtree is a busy man, and I have my duties to Queen's College. I suggest that we finish our business as speedily as possible."

"Nothing that I can do or say," laughed the Squire, "appears to have any weight with any of you. I give in. Since I am thus discredited, let me at least know how my fool of a nephew stands in your regard. Is he, or is he not, mentioned in this Almago's will?" To which Imogene replied: "Mister Antony Cobtree here is representing my mother and myself in English Law. I have already translated my dear father's last testament to him from the Spanish, which he has put into legal terms in English. As your nephew's guardian—and may I say that we are both very attached to your nephew, sir?—it is only right that in his behalf you should hear my father's last wishes concerning him. Mister Cobtree, will you proceed?" Tony Cobtree afterwards confessed that he not only enjoyed the official situation, in which he found himself, but went out of his way to sound the deepest dryness of the legal phrases which he uttered. And in this vanity he might well be excused, since it was the very first case he had undertaken.

Solemnly he read through the terms of the late Spaniard's will, which he had turned into English Law jargon from the translation supplied by Imogene. But if he had thought to be tiresome to the Squire of Iffley, he was mistaken, for the bully drank in the news of the Spanish ladies' wealth with avidity, and the more wealthy they seemed to grow according to the young lawyer's statement, so much the more did the Squire ogle the beautiful Se—orita.

The part of the will which touched the Squire's nephew stated that the vessel which the deceased provided and fitted out for Nicholas Tappitt should be still held in commission with the said Nicholas Tappitt as sailing-master, and that after payment from each or any voyage, such profits accruing from the same should be divided into equal portions, and paid the one to the sailingmaster and the other to the deceased's daughter Imogene. This statement concluded the business, and Cobtree asked if anyone had any comment to make.

At which the Squire got to his feet and, much to Doctor Syn's annoyance, took Imogene's hand and kissed her fingertips.

"It seems, then," he said with a laugh, "that my wretched nephew will at least have the felicity to be connected closely with you in the way of business.

Will you object to that, Doctor Syn? Or will you be sensible enough to pocket the profit which my nephew's trading brings to your wife? I warrant it will be higher than the stipend of a parson."

"I think we need detain the Squire of Iffley no longer," rapped out the attorney.

"I will gladly accompany him downstairs," added Doctor Syn, "for by the looks of it the crowd had grown even larger, and I venture to think that he will need a little protection on the way to his coach."

"We will both accompany him, with your leave," added Cobtree.

The Squire surveyed the young men haughtily.

"I have not the least fear of your rabble, gentlemen, but I shall

welcome your company to the door, since I have that to say to you
which I should prefer the ladies not to hear. Madame, I am your
humble servant." (This is the Se—ora.) "And as to your daughter's
rejection of my nephew in favour of this young scholar—well, I shall
have a good deal to say to my nephew on the subject which will not
be to his liking, for I could never tolerate a failure. But for Heaven's
sake, Madame, see that your daughter contemplates well what she
is doing before condemning her whole life to a dull English
parsonage. I shall be happy to welcome you both at Iffley whenever
you care to honour me. Now, gentlemen, at your service." The
Squire's attitude, his insults and his reputation prepared Doctor
Syn for what was to follow, and as he led the way down the stairs
he decided what course he would take in retaliation. Tony Cobtree
followed with his hand on his sword.

What both the young men suspected would happen came
quickly enough.

They knew the initiative was in the Squire's hands, and he
took it highhandedly. Ignoring the growl of protest against him
from the crowd, he turned and faced the two young Marshmen. A
step below them on the porch he looked up at young Cobtree.

"Do I owe you any small fee for your service?" he asked, with
one hand in his breeches pocket. "I find I have plenty of small
change about me."

"You owe me nothing," replied Cobtree coldly. "In my
professional capacity I was acting for the ladies, not for you."

"As for you, sir," went on the Squire, turning fiercely upon
Doctor Syn, "since you have taken it upon yourself to interfere with
my business, I shall make a point of interfering with yours."

"Since I have no interest in you at all," replied Doctor Syn, "I
fail to see in what way I could have interfered."

"I call it the grossest interference," went on the Squire, "the
way you have crept in behind my nephew's back, knowing him to
be safe away at sea, and then with your smooth tongue to have
seduced the mind of a rich, beautiful, but ignorant girl who should
have been his wife. Well, marry her if you can, but you will first
answer this"—and with the back of his hand he struck the parson
in the mouth.

Although the blood trickled down from his lip where the
Squire's ring had cut it, Doctor Syn appeared deadly calm. Raising
his right hand to check the angry murmur of the crowd behind the
Squire, he said:

"I will answer you at once, though not in the way you expect.

You have just struck a cowardly blow, knowing full well that it would not be seemly for me to meet you with either barrel or blade. But I have a man's heart beneath my black coat, and I take a blow from no one as despicable as you. So down with you into the gutter, where you belong." Very deliberately Doctor Syn began to remove his clerical coat. But ere he could accomplish this, the Squire had drawn his sword, and with the flat of the blade struck the parson with all his force upon his shoulder. In a second Tony Cobtree's sword was drawn, and with a "Coward, en garde", he engaged the Squire.

While hoots of "Shame!" and "Tear him!" arose from the crowd, Doctor Syn's voice rang above all, crying, "This is my quarrel, Tony." At the same time he leapt, dropping his coat upon the steps, and as he turned the blades with the impact of his body, he struck up with his left fist and caught the Squire with all his force upon the jaw. The sudden impact seemed to lift the heavy bully off his feet, and down he went backwards with a sickening thud as his head struck the cobble-stones.

It was then that the crowd pounced, like encouraged terriers upon a rat. The Squire's sword was wrested from his grasp, and sent crashing through the windows of his coach. At the same time the wretched footman had been dragged from the horses' heads and thrown to the mob, while others seized the reins. The armed coachman, assailed from back and front, fired his blunderbuss into the air, and then gave in for very fear. He was dragged from his box. His wrists were lashed behind him with the corded frogs that they ripped from his gorgeous uniformed coat. His wig was torn off and stuffed into his mouth as a gag, tied with its own ribbon.

Despite the efforts of both Doctor Syn and Cobtree to save him, the Squire of Iffley was lifted up by the infuriated townsmen and bundled into his coach.

The coachman and footman were pushed in after him, and then, amidst wild yells of derision, they led the horses through the Market, and into solemn procession as far as Magdalen Bridge. Here, as the young men were afterwards to learn, the frightened animals were left to their own devices. A strong flick from the long whip which someone stole, and the coach went off in mad career, swaying and ungoverned. The wretched inmates of the vehicle must have thanked their stars that the horses knew the way, for they pulled up panting and kicking at the closed iron gates, until the gate-keeper came out and led them through. The thanks this fellow received at the hands of his master for having rescued him and the servants was a stroke over the mouth, so that his lip was cut similarly to Doctor Syn's. He then threatened him with dismissal, but then, remembering that the rascal knew Doctor Syn and might yet be useful in trapping him, he gave him a guinea, and bade him visit the house after dinner in order to plan the winning of further guineas. And behind them in Oxford the Giles' Fair went on, and in the upper parlour of White Friars it was Tony who said:

"We have not heard the last of our Squire of Iffley, I fear."

"The rascal is going to be undone for this affair," replied Syn, "and I rather think that I shall have most hand in it."

"What do you intend to do?" Imogene noted the grave anxiety on the lawyer's face, and it frightened her.

Doctor Syn paused to think and then continued, "I propose that you and I shall pay a call upon the Chancellor, and over a bottle of his excellent port shall give him our version of today's affair. What do you say?"

"Why, that we could no nothing better," cried Tony, much relieved.

"That is settled, then," said Syn, "and I propose also that till then we dismiss the Squire of Iffley from our minds, and think on happier things."

Chapter 5. The Abduction

Although his jaw ached prodigiously from the result of the blow inflicted upon it by Doctor Syn, and although he ached from head to foot from his fall and the manhandling he had afterwards received, the Squire of Iffley lost no time in planning his revenge. He decided that this could best be served by first striking at Doctor Syn through the beautiful Spanish girl. If he could kidnap both the mother and daughter from the house in St. Giles', and get them spirited away to his own mansion at Iffley, he felt that he could hold them prisoners until they consented to all his wishes.

He summoned the gate-keeper to whom he had given the blow and the guinea.

"I presume, Mister Cragg," he whispered, as the gate-keeper stood before him at the dining-room table, "that you have had a full account of what happened this morning in St. Giles'? No doubt my carriage servants have given you the most graphic and, I dare swear, exaggerated version of the disadvantage I was put to, and in which they shared. Is that so?"

"I have heard that things did not go well with your honour," replied the man. "In fact the state of your honour's coach told me that the cards must have fallen damned bad."

"And so they did," admitted the Squire, filling his glass with port. "But a gentleman of spirit should never get down-hearted at the continual falling of bad cards, for it always comes to your own deal at last."

"With a good ace tucked up one's sleeve," chuckled the man.

"And why not?" laughed the Squire. "Maybe I lost this morning, but it is my deal now, and those I play against will be astonished at the number of aces I shall have up my sleeve, and if by your help I win the game I mean to play, you shall have twenty guineas in your pocket. Now listen carefully, and I will tell you how I wish the cards to fall." Whereupon the Squire unfolded his scheme.

Mister Cragg had no difficulty in watching White Friars, nor in recognizing his master's victims. There was Doctor Syn, whom he had met already, with his arm round the beautiful Spanish girl. There was the elder Spanish lady, her mother, and the other two at the open window he knew must be the lawyer and the lady he was wooing in the Woodstock Road. The crowded booths and stalls opposite the house lent him an easy concealment. As compensation for his weary wait, he watched the happiness upon the lovers' faces, and gloated over the contrasting emotions that were in store for them.

Earlier than he expected, he saw the whole party withdraw from the window, and began to congratulate himself that the gentlemen were so soon retiring. In this, however, he was doomed to disappointment, for it was only the lawyer and his lady who appeared at the front door, with Doctor Syn bidding them farewell.

But it was at parting that Cragg heard the lawyer say: "I shall be back within the hour, Christopher, and then we'll wend along together to the Chancellor.

He sits up late enough, the old rascal, and will welcome us to drink his port."

"Well, Tony," laughed Doctor Syn, "linger if you will upon the way, but hurry all you can upon your return, for, as you know, the Se—ora likes to retire to bed in good time."

"Within the hour without fail," replied Tony Cobtree, taking the hand of his lady and placing it under his arm, as they threaded their way through the packed merry-makers in St. Giles'.

So Mister Cragg had to exert his patience for yet another hour. However, Tony Cobtree was as good as his word, and better, for in half an hour he was back, and Cragg had no more waiting, for the two men immediately left the house on their way to the Chancellor's.

Although he knew their destination, Cragg followed them to make sure. He knew that they were not returning that night to White Friars, for he had heard Doctor Syn say to the Spanish girl, "I will be round for breakfast in the morning." So when he saw them both disappear into the Chancellor's house he knew that it was safe, as far as they were concerned, to put the plot in motion.

But he lingered on the way back so that dusk should give place to night. Having seen that the carriage was ready outside St. Giles', in order to avoid the crowds, he leisurely walked towards White Friars. There he waited until the candles in the upper parlour were extinguished. He saw the light of bedroom candles being carried into another room, and then he rang the bell vigorously. The housekeeper, after some delay, opened the door on the chain, and he handed in a note, saying that the matter was very urgent and he would wait instructions. A few minutes later he was admitted into the hall, and found, just as the Squire had hoped, that the Spanish girl had readily fallen into the trap. Although her manner was calm, her eyes were bathed in tears, as she asked Cragg whether he had seen the accident. He told her, "No," but he had seen the unfortunate gentlemen afterwards and had helped his master to lift him into a carriage, which was now waiting to convey her to the house, which was on the outskirts of the town.

"I will just go up and hasten my mother," she said, "and we will start immediately. Where is the carriage you mention?" Cragg told her it was beyond the crowd, some two hundred yards distant, and that he would escort them to it.

Five minutes later Cragg was escorting them through the crowds, and the carriage was reached. Seeing that they were so full of the calamity, that no suspicion of foul play had entered their heads, Cragg decided to climb on to the box rather than ride inside with the ladies, which he thought they would resent.

Once the horses were off, he knew there would be no stopping, for at such a time the roads would be free.

Only once, and towards the end of the journey, did the girl put her head out of the carriage window and ask how much farther.

"We are nearly there, madame," answered Cragg, giving the driver a jocular nudge in his ribs.

A few minutes later they turned through the gates, which, to save trouble and delay, he had left open, and were sweeping up the drive at a gallop. The hall door was open for their reception, and the butler ushered them in. He led them into the dining-room, after closing the heavy hall door, and said that if they would wait there a minute he would inform his master, who was now consulting with the physician in the sick man's room.

It was then that Imogene heard two noises which puzzled her for the moment. The sound of the carriage driving away, and the bolting and chaining of the hall door. But before any suspicion had time to take root in her mind the butler returned with an explanation. He reported that if the sufferer could be kept alive through the night, he had hopes for his recovery. At the moment he had drifted into unconsciousness, but directly he revived to his senses the young lady would be permitted to see him. Two visitors the doctor could not allow, but as the reverend gentleman kept asking for Imogene, the sight of her would perhaps bring him a little peace. Since the case was desperate, the servants had orders to accommodate the ladies in a bedroom adjoining, in case they were needed in the night. The butler said he had been told to ask them if they would accept this hospitality, and whether they would care for a glass of wine before proceeding upstairs. This they both declined. Imogene saying that she would see her mother to the room, and hoped they were not causing too much inconvenience, and she added that if the lady of the house was at liberty she would like to thank her for all they were doing.

"My lady will visit you in a few moments in the bedroom," replied the butler. "At the moment she is helping the doctor with the reverend gentleman's bandages. I will give instructions for the lady's-maid to wait upon you and to see that you have all that you require. Will you follow me, please?" He led them upstairs, across a wide landing to an open bedroom door. They went in and found it old-fashioned and comfortable.

"I will inform my lady," said the butler as he closed the door. In a minute he was back again and whispered: "The reverend gentleman has recovered consciousness. Will the young lady come at once, please?"

"Yes, go, my dear," whispered her mother. "I will wait for you here. I hope he is better." Imogene noticed as she passed through the bedroom door that the key was in the outside of the lock, but as all her thoughts were set on comforting her lover, she saw nothing suspicious in that. She closed the door herself, and followed the butler down a short flight of stairs, along a corridor with a door at the far end. This the butler opened, and signed for her to go through.

"Thank you," she whispered, and went in on tiptoe.

Her first view of the room, which was brilliantly lighted with candles, astonished her, for instead of the bedroom she had expected she found herself in a spacious oak-panelled sitting-room with a great round card-table in the centre. Before she had recovered from her surprise, she heard the door close behind her, and turning saw not the butler, who had gone, but a richly dressed gentleman locking the door on the inside and putting the key in his pocket.

"What is the meaning of this, sir?" she asked. "And where is Doctor Syn?" The Squire of Iffley turned and faced her with a chuckle. Instantly she recognized him, and gasped with terror.

"Quite right, my dear girl," he said. "You are trapped. Your mother is locked in her room, so if you scream you will but add to her alarm. Since Doctor Syn, who is back in Oxford all the time, thought fit to make you scorn my hospitality, I have been forced to go my own way to work. You are now at Iffley in my Manor, and here you will stay till you have consented to all my demands."

"And what are they, sir?" she asked haughtily.

"First that you will discontinue this absurd love affair with Doctor Syn," he answered.

"In order that you may force me to marry your nephew, sir?" she demanded.

"Spit me, no," he laughed. "There is no love lost between us, I assure you, and why should I help him to what I most desire for myself? I would rather leave my money and estate to our children, my dear, than to that fool of a nephew who has failed to carry you off."

"Our children?" repeated the girl in horror. "How dare you even think of such a thing?"

"For the same reason that I shall accomplish it. I want you for my wife, and willynilly you shall marry me. Of that I am so certain that I urge you for your own sake not to fight against it. Many a woman would envy you. I am a bachelor, and rich. I am not without accomplishments. No man in the country rides harder, fights harder, or drinks harder. I can hold my own with much younger men. And although I have never married, women admire me because of my settled determination. Whatever I want, I get. So school your mind, little Miss, to forget this young parson, and accept my wooing."

"I shall do nothing of the sort," replied Imogene.

"Oh yes, you will, because I shall force you to it. I have the means here to compel your obedience. That is why I have kidnapped your mother. You will not care to see her starved and tortured, while I surround you with every luxury? If you refuse to be sensible, I shall strike at you through her. We will talk now for an hour or so, and then unless you relent, her persecution will commence, and I warrant her screams will move you."

"Doctor Syn will suspect you," said Imogene coldly. "He will come and free me when he finds that we have gone from White Friars. He will know that the story of his accident was a base lie."

"Of course he will," laughed the Squire. "He'll know it tonight. I have written him a letter to his Chambers. The servant who brought you your letter is now on his way to deliver another to the parson. In it I have stated that you have changed your mind, and have, with your mother's consent, arranged for yourself a happier match than to become a parson's wife. Of course he may believe this.

If he does we shall not be troubled with him."

"He will not believe it," replied Imogene. "How can you think it?"

"To be quite frank, I never did," said the Squire, with a smile. "I think— nay, I hope—he will come up here. And when he does he will not leave here alive. Unless, of course, you so convince him that my letter is the truth. In that case I will spare him, and you will have the satisfaction of saving his life. I confess that my words will sound conceited, but I could not help crowing a good deal over the success of my revenge. Now will you drink a glass of wine?"

"Nothing," she answered coldly.

"Will you come and sit beside me on this comfortable settee?"

"I will not."

"Very well," he went on in his bantering tone, "you may stand there while I sit and drink. I am perfectly content to gloat upon you for an hour. Then you will not only be willing to sit, but you will sit upon my knee and sip the wine from my glass."

"I shall do nothing of the kind, you conceited devil," she said.

"Oh yes, you will. In an hour. In one hour precisely. Do you know why."

"I do not care to know."

"And yet it is my duty to tell you," he replied pleasantly. "I must save my future wife from shock. And in one hour you will hear your mother's first scream of pain and terror. I have servants here who are very expert at that kind of treatment. There is a clock. Watch it. One hour." And he sipped his wine and watched her standing there.

Chapter 6. The Duel

Now, the moment Cragg had seen the butler close the hall door safely upon the ladies he proceeded immediately to Queen's College, aroused the porter and inquired whether Doctor Syn had yet retired to bed. The porter informed him that the Reverend Gentleman was abroad at the house of the Chancellor. Cragg said that he had a very important letter to be delivered to the Reverend Gentleman and would the porter be seeing him on his return? The porter assured Cragg that he would, since it was his duty to unlock the gate to anyone abroad after closing hour. So Cragg left the note, crossed the road, went down a side street, came back by another, and waited to watch in the shadows.

Both Cobtree and Syn stayed a long time with the Chancellor, who had been delighted to see them, since many a rumour of the adventure in St. Giles' had reached him, and he was anxious to have the truth of the affair. The young men were relieved to find him very sympathetic, and indeed entirely upon their side.

He agreed with them that the neighbourhood would be the cleaner if cleared of such a rascal, but he did not desire any scandal to fall upon the University. He pointed out that whereas Mr. Cobtree was perfectly entitled to take up the bully's challenge, since he was free of the ties of studentship, Doctor Syn was in different case.

To this Doctor Syn had raised objections. "Do you mean, sir, that because one is an official of the University, any bully can insult one with impunity?"

"I mean this, my good young Doctor," the old man replied. "No man of sense could call in question the honour of anyone in Holy Orders who declined to give satisfaction, or ask it, from a noted duellist. You have chosen a profession which must ever put the Word before the sword."

"And yet, sir," argued the Doctor, "Christ Himself whipped the moneylenders from the Temple."

"I am not saying that I should not be the first to applaud you were you to give the rascal a good thrashing. But should we once countenance duelling within College walls, why, we should have every high-spirited young gentleman under our charge killing one another. No, Doctor Syn, you have shown quite enough of your mettle by knocking the bully into the roadway, and my advice is to let it rest at that." After an hour or so, the mellowness of the good old man's excellent advice and admirable wine imparted itself to the spirits of both the young gentlemen, so that when they bade him farewell, and walked into the night air, each was desirous of seeing the other to his home.

"You are a guest, Tony," said Doctor Syn, "and have already kept your future relatives up too long. I will walk there with you."

"And have you no regard for your College gate-keeper?" laughed Cobtree. "I told my in-laws I should be late, and they have entrusted me with their house key. I will therefore walk with you to Queen's, and drink a good-night glass with you. What do you say?"

"I can hardly refuse my best friend hospitality," laughed Syn.

And thus it was that Fate gave Doctor Syn a valued ally in a great adventure for no sooner had they rung the porter's bell than the Squire's note was handed to the Doctor.

He read it by the light of the lantern in the lodge, and as he read, his friend saw his face veiled over with determined rage.

"What is wrong, Christopher?" he asked.

Doctor Syn crumpled the letter in his hand and, bringing his fist down with a crash upon the porter's desk, cried out, "That settles it! Either I or that rascal dies tonight. The Chancellor did not guess at this. Read it and wait here. There is something I must fetch from my chambers." Cobtree did not obey, but with the letter in his hand hurried after his friend, and when the chamber door was unlocked and Doctor Syn had lighted a candle in the cosy and familiar study, Tony smoothed the paper and read. By the time he had finished it, with many a gasp of horror and surprise, his friend stood before him in a long cloak.

"This is a wicked lie," cried Cobtree, flourishing the letter. "Let us go to White Friars, where no doubt we shall find the dear ladies are sleeping safely.

This is but a trap to get you to Iffley."

"By gad, Tony, you are right, I never thought of that. Come with me to St.

Giles', and if they are not there—well, then, I am for Iffley and the rascal's blood."

"Of course they will be there," said Tony. "How could he have dragged them from the house?"

"Well, if he has," said Syn between clenched teeth, "I have this about me that will rescue them," and drawing back his cloak he tapped the hilt of a long sword. "It was my father's, who was but with the Prince in '45. He took it from my father's dead hand. Aye, the old lawyer died game enough, and so will I if needs be. Come on. If they have gone, I'll get a horse at Hobson's. And if they are there I'll get it just the same and teach this rogue that parsons are first of all gentlemen. The Chancellor may groan, but this night I fight a duel. At least come with me to St. Giles', but after that I go alone."

"Come along, then," replied Tony grimly. "We'll get along there as quickly as we can, and after we will get two horses from Hobson's." And so the two friends hurried from Queen's to St. Giles', where all was quiet, as the Fair had closed.

Now, owing to the fact that the landlady at White Friars had been extremely anxious as to the fate of Doctor Syn, the two young gentlemen found a light burning downstairs, and on their knock upon the door it was immediately opened. Although very glad to find the Doctor alive and able, when she had told them about the ladies under her charge and had read the contents of the Squire of Iffley's letter, she was in a sore state of panic, in which Doctor Syn and Tony had to leave her, since their haste was urgent in order to rescue the ladies from what they knew would be unspeakable torture.

As they ran toward Hobson's stables, Doctor Syn begged Tony to go home and leave the rest to him, which, of course, Tony refused to do. But it was not until Doctor Syn found himself galloping neck to neck over Magdalen Bridge alongside his friend that he realized nothing could shake off Tony Cobtree from the perilous adventure.

"To the gates of Iffley, I suppose?" cried Tony, spurring on.

"No," retorted the Doctor. "I have a better plan. We will pick up on our way another ally against the rascal. We will rouse the farmer I told you about, because this is to be war to the death, and the more upon our side the better our generalship against this rogue, who will have a host of retainers at his back.

From what I told you, I think this farmer will not hang back now."

"Aye," cried Tony, riding hard. "If we ride to the gates of Iffley they will be prepared for you, but if this fellow can ferry us over the Isis in his boat and land us there upon the Iffley estate, we shall attack perhaps with more surprise." Although the hour was very late, the young men were fortunate in finding a light in the cowshed, where the farmer was attending to a sick animal. He recognized Doctor Syn immediately, and after hearing that their errand was in the quest of revenge, was at once eager not only to help, but to take an active part in the affair. In the space of a few minutes Hobson's horses were stabled, and he was leading them towards the meadow bank where he moored a fishingboat.

"I bring a loaded pistol for the cause, sir," he said. "I am no gentleman and cannot use a sword, but if you two should fail to kill this vermin, believe me, gentlemen, I can shoot straight. And now, please tell me how you intend to act when we touch the farther bank."

"Proceed to the house, and kick up hell till we get in, of course," said Syn.

"I have a better plan than that," replied the farmer. "A secret that for years has been a source of comfort to me. You may have heard of Charles Herman.

He is the most skilful cabinet-maker in Oxford."

"Very well," said Syn. "He does a lot of work for the colleges."

"He is my brother-in-law," went on the farmer. "A year or so back he was called in by the Squire yonder to open up a sliding panel in the great oak room on the first floor which the scoundrel uses for his gaming. This panel, as our Charles discovered, leads by a flight of winding steps to the old water-gate. In his father's time it had been closed, but no doubt the present Squire has found good use for it. There have been bodies recovered from the Isis before now over which the coroner has pronounced 'Suicide' or 'Accidental death by drowning'.

On each occasion, Charles and I thought differently. The poor victims had no doubt fallen foul of Bully Tappitt. Charles repaired the secret spring which operates on both sides of the door, and being an expert locksmith too, he had to make a new key to fit the water-gate. After the tragedy to my daughter, Charles told me of this secret way, and I learned that he had not destroyed the mould from which he made the key. I begged him to make another, which he did, and gave to me. I have it always here against my heart. It is a large key, but the feel of it has ever been a joy to me. The knowledge that at any time I had the means to surprise that devil has made my heart sing for sheer delight. I have used it many times, and listened at the panel. But on each occasion he had company, and I needed him alone. Sometimes in the dead of night I have let myself through the panel, which Charles had made to slide so silently, and have stood in the oak room gloating on what would one night happen there. I noted that he kept his duelling pistols there, and they were loaded. I hoped to use one of these instead of mine own, for the murder would then seem suicide. Well, gentlemen, we will use the key now, and with God's help rescue your ladies and deal with the Squire." Silently they got into the boat, and the farmer took the oars, rowing with caution against any noise. As they passed the Squire's boat-house they heard a man's voice singing a bawdy song, and saw a light in a window above it.

"It is the water-man," whispered the farmer. "He drinks himself into the early hours like his master. He will not trouble us." The water-gate was round a bend of the river, some fifty yards from the boat-house, and the only spot where the house itself touched the river. With a final pull the farmer shipped his oars carefully and crawled into the bow, where he crouched with a short boat-hook. Without a word he pointed above his head, and the young men knew that the large mullioned window lighted up was the oak room for which they were bound. The farmer eased the boat gently to the wall and made fast to a mooring-ring. He then crawled on to the gateway step and motioned the others to follow. There was no noise save the gentle lapping of the river beneath the boat.

The water-gate was fitted with a heavy oak door, iron-studded. The farmer produced his key from his shirt, and by the time the door had swung silently into the darkness the young men were standing close behind him. Cautiously they all entered, and the farmer shut the door behind him. Step by step they mounted, the farmer first, since he knew where to find the secret spring. Doctor Syn next, and Cobtree last. After completing the first turn of the turret, the farmer put out his hand behind him to call a halt while he listened. It was then that Syn turned to his friend and whispered:

"I would have been happy to see you clear of this adventure, Tony. For your parents' sake, and for your lady. But oh, man, I am yet glad to have you with me. But it is first of all my quarrel!" The farmer turned and warned them not to whisper. Then once more they mounted up. Syn calculated that they had completed three full turns of the turret, and by the sound of a man's voice knew they were reaching the top, when the farmer turned and whispered the order, "Back." they retreated three steps, and only just in time, for suddenly the turret steps were flooded with light, and the hitherto murmuring voice of the man arose loud and clear, showing that the panel was open wide. The farmer levelled his pistol, and the young men's hands went to their sword-hilts.

"It leads to the river," said the voice of the Squire. "I show it to you just to prove how completely you are in my power. In a few minutes it will be time for you to hear your mother scream again. My rascals are punctual. They delight in their work. If, as you tried to threaten when you heard the last scream, your mother were to die of shock, her body would be carried down these steps and with a bag of stones around her neck she would sink to the bottom of the river.

You know that you can stop your mother's terror at will. You have only to consent to me, and all will be happy for her. And for you, too, if you only knew it. I am something of a good lover, my dear. After the next scream or groan, whichever it may be, you will hear them more rapidly, for my instructions are to increase the dose as the night wears on. Why not let the old girl alone, my dear? She could lie upon the bed and cry herself to sleep if you will only be kind to me. Why not give in? Eventually you must, and you will save her so much pain. Listen. There. A moan. Do you hear? Ah yes, and now?" A piercing scream arose from a distant part of the house. Doctor Syn tried to push past the farmer, but he held him firmly back.

The Squire's voice went on: "It is no use you running to that door, my dear. I have the key in my pocket. What a horrid scream that was! She must be suffering. How can you suffer it? Now obey me, child. Undo your little bodice. I have a wish to kiss you on the shoulders." Once more Doctor Syn tried to push by the farmer. But the latter was a strong man, and, being above the parson on the steps, had the advantage.

Thrusting his pistol into his side pocket, he used one hand in keeping the Doctor back and the other was pressed hard over his mouth to prevent him from making a noise.

It was then that they heard Imogene's voice for the first time.

"God will have no mercy on you when my Christopher, Doctor Syn, arrives.

He will kill you, and God will bless him for the deed."

"I have tried to be merciful to you," replied the Squire. "I have been patient too long. Why should I wait when my lips are burning for you? I am going to take you in my arms." At this moment, and just as Doctor Syn was about to hurl himself at the farmer, whose strong arms had pressed him back, there came a sharp knocking on the locked door at the far end of the room.

"That will be news of your mother, no doubt," said the Squire. "We will open and see. But in case you are tempted to run down these dusty steps, we will close the panel. Not that you could get far, because below there is a locked door that leads to the river."

The Squire closed the panel as he spoke, and as his heavy strides crossed the room the three avengers climbed the remaining steps. The farmer had his hand upon the secret spring, and Doctor Syn whispered him to open it.

"Wait till whoever has come has gone," cautioned the farmer.

When the Squire unlocked the door, Imogene gave a gasp of horror, for there stood before her an enormous man stripped to the waist and holding a huge pair of blacksmith's pincers.

"Well, fool, what is it?" asked the Squire.

"That last nip I gave her put her out," growled the brute. "What shall I do? Wait for her to wake up, or go on as you ordered?"

"Throw a jugful of water over her, throw her on the bed, and lock her in for the night," ordered the Squire. "Leave the key in her lock, in case I wish to view her. And give the strictest orders to the servants that I am not to be disturbed until the morning. Under no circumstances are any of you to set foot in this wing of the house. You will mount guard in the main hall, with the stable-lads. If this Doctor Syn should come clammering at the doors, see first who comes with him. If he is alone, or merely with his lawyer friend, admit him, and deal with him. You will be more than enough to settle with them.

Have cords to lash them up, and put them down in the old dungeon vaults till morning. It may be I shall kill him in the morning—both of them if they come.

That depends upon this little beauty here. If the loving is to be all on my side tonight, the parson has preached his last sermon. Now go, and don't disturb me till the morning, no matter what shrieks and screams you hear from this part of the house. Understand?"

"I understand, your honour, and wish you a very good night. I think your honour will have it, too." And with a grin of appreciation at the terrified girl, he went out, closing the door behind him.

The Squire poured himself out another glass of wine.

"Just one more to wish your mother a happier state, which is in your hands, and then—" He drank, set down the glass and eyed her. "And now, my dear, unless you prefer to wait upon yourself, you will permit my clumsy fingers to act the lady's-maid. That tempting little bodice must be unhooked. Yes. Now." The wine mounted to his brain as he lurched toward her.

"Have pity!" she pleaded.

"It is you who are cruel," he said. "Your beauty tortures me. Must I take you without consent? It will be worse for your mother if I do. Come here, you ravishing devil, and let me kiss you down to Hell."

"Where you are bound for now." These words were rapped out in a cold voice behind him.

The Squire, who had seized the girl in his strong embrace, swung round, as what he saw drained the blood from his heated cheeks. He stood there swaying, ashen pale, with terror in his eyes. He seemed incapable of movement, but just stared at the two cloaked figures who were standing there with drawn swords.

For the moment Imogene could not believe her sight. She had forgotten the secret panel. The mysterious appearance of her lover and his friend to her was something of the supernatural. Doctor Syn saw that the Squire was equally mystified, and calmly he set him right.

"We are no ghosts, my Bully," he said icily. "Indeed, you will find us very flesh and blood. You have insulted us both. You will fight us both, though something tells me there will be no need for Mr. Cobtree to engage you. You are a bully, a coward, a liar and a cheat. And you will fight now, and in this room, which you have so carefully left undisturbed till dawn." With an effort the Squire seemed to shake his huge body into some confidence. He knew at least that he was a match for most in a duel.

"May I ask," he said coldly, "the name of the servant who has betrayed my secret panel to you, parson? For after I have dealt with you, with both of you, I shall deal with him. I pay good wages for services, but only death for betrayal."

"It is not your servants, but your sins, that have betrayed you," went on Doctor Syn. "I wonder now if you recollect among your victims a certain lovely girl called Esther Sommers. Ah; I see you do. She died of the shame she suffered at your hands. Since God is shortly to judge you for that, I will not dwell on that girl's tragedy. But I wish to point out your own stupidity. You did not know that Charles Herman was her uncle, did you?"

"And who the hell is he?" demanded the Squire.

"The cabinet-maker and locksmith who repaired this panel behind me," explained Syn. "You were very stupid not to see that he destroyed the mould from which he made the key to the water-gate. From it he made another key, and gave it to the father of

Esther Sommers. We have made good use of that key tonight. You
see, there comes a time when the most evil man can mock God no
more."

"Don't preach, but fight!" cried the Squire.

"I shall be at your service in a moment, sir," replied Syn. He
turned to Imogene, who had been so overcome with grief that she
had been unable to move. "My beloved, thank God, Who guided us
here to rescue you in time." As she flung herself sobbing into his
arms, the Squire took three swift strides towards a cabinet on
which lay his case of pistols. But Tony Cobtree was there first, with
his sword at the other's breast.

"Take your hand from that box, sir," he cried, "or by God I'll
spit you like an ox! Get back!"

"I was merely preparing for the fight, sir. You may examine the
pistols if you wish."

"We fight with steel," said Syn finally. He then turned again to
Imogene and added, "Do you know where your mother is, so that
we may relieve her of anxiety?"

"Yes," replied Imogene. "Let us go to her at once. And then,
Christopher, let us go and leave this devil. Let us leave him to the
law to deal with. Why should you risk your life?"

"Because I believe that God has appointed me to kill him." He
then looked at his friend and added, "Tony, do you take Imogene
to her mother, for I have my duty here, which will be no sight for
ladies." Tony shook his head. "I am sorry, old friend. But, knowing
the man's reputation, I feel obligated too stay here and see fair
fight."

"This is my home, gentlemen," cried the Squire. "And I'll brook
your insults no longer. Let us either hear the clash of steel or the
crack of artillery, and be done with it. Then I shall be at liberty to
enjoy the fresh beauty of this ravisher." In two strides Syn was at
him, and with all his strength he smote him on his unhealed
wound upon the jaw, cutting it open till the blood fell in a red
cascade upon his cravat.

"I'll kill you for this!" hissed the Squire.

"I ask nothing better than that you should try," replied the
parson.

There was no question of Imogene's mother then, for the
Squire unhooked two duelling-swords from above the fireplace and
placed them, hilts from him, on the gaming table.

"Choose!" he cried.

"I choose my own sword to kill you with," replied the parson.

"It was returned to me by a man of Romney Marsh who took it from my father's dead hand at Culloden Field. Your own blade may be the longer, for all I care, but I fight you with my father's sword. Are you afraid at last? It is the first time you have met a better man?" Now, for his father's sword Syn had a great affection. As a matter of sentiment he had not only kept it clean and sharp, but he had trained his hand to use it as his father's son, and despite his cloth of peace he had taken it daily to the fencing-school for exercise. Thus it was that the Squire of Iffley was unpleasantly surprised when, having selected a weapon to match his opponent's, he found a blade opposing him that proved a brain within its temper.

It may have been a full minute that the blades slithered and clanked, but in that minute the Squire knew that he would have to use his utmost skill and be aided by fortune in order to break down the other's guard. He therefore called a halt by crying out:"A moment, Mister Parson. If we are fighting to the death and in my house, I would wish that all things were fair. I see you know something of fence. Well, as sportsmen let us enjoy the other's skill before one of us shall fall. Suppose we both remove our coats and vests, roll up our sleeves, drink our last drink, maybe, and fall to it again?"

"As you wish, sir," replied the parson, and then to Imogene, "We shall not keep your dear mother long in suspense. In a few minutes she will be avenged." Meanwhile Cobtree had taken advantage of the break to better the duelling space. He pulled aside the big gaming-table, and placed the movable candelabras facing one another in the centre of the room. This, with the help of the hanging chandeliers, concentrated the light into the centre of the oak floor.

He then rolled aside the heavy rugs, and was about to move the wine-table, when the Squire interrupted.

"We will drink before we fight," he said. "Although there is nothing but hate between us, I will at least offer you that much hospitality. I would see no one bound for hell or heaven lacking a drink."

"For us, sir, no," replied Syn, who had already stripped himself of coat and vest and clerical cravat, and rolled up his shirtsleeves. "Mr. Cobtree and myself are only in the habit of drinking with gentlemen. From your appearance you have drunk already more than is good for your safety, and if you will permit me to preach once more to your advantage, I should counsel you to abstain from more, since you will need all your wits and skill to hold your own against my death-thrusts. Swill if you will, swine, and then join blades again. Tony, will you oblige me by moving that pistol-case to the far end of the room behind my back?"

"You think I would take an ill advantage of you?" snarled the Squire.

"Think?" re-echoed Doctor Syn. "I know. I take no foolish chances with a liar and a cheat. Come, sir, drink if you must, and let us be done with it once and for all." Foolishly the Squire drank straight from the bottle's neck till it was done.

Dr. Syn watched him and said aloud, "You fool! that last drink has delivered you into my hands. But do me the grace to own I warned you. Come, sir.

Defend yourself as best you can." This time the Squire selected another blade of longer reach, to which Cobtree objected, but Doctor Syn waved him aside and touched blades in warning.

Furiously the Squire attacked, and as the minutes sped to the ring of steel his fury increased, because he found in the young parson a swordsman the like of which he had never met before. Their methods were different, for the Squire fought with a dashing ferocity, showing a lithe agility remarkable in a man of such heavy bulk. But the parson met each fiery attack with a rock-like defense, and although retreating slowly before the licking steel, he seemed to do so with cool deliberation. Right down the room, the Squire like a fierce whirlwind drove him, till at last the parson felt the panelling touch his back.

With a hideous misgiving for this friend's safety, Cobtree cried out, "Attack!" It was then that Syn smiled and shook his head, while the Squire doubled the speed of his attack, determined to keep his opponent pinned against the wall until he could break through his defence. The Squire had now the advantage of the lights behind him, and this he meant to keep until he could deliver the death-thrust. But the same thought was in the mind of Doctor Syn, and despite the rapidity of the licking thrusts, his voice rose above the continual clash and slithers of the steel.

Calmly he said, "I think we will get back into the light again." With the same deliberation that he had used in his retreat, He now as calmly advanced, slowly but surely, foot by foot.

To Cobtree's practised eye it now seemed as though the Squire was rebounding from the heavy impact of his own attacks, for though the parson steadily advanced with an uncanny assurance, he still fought only on defence, checking each lightning lunge with his impregnable barrier of steel.

The Squire's livid face began to change from red rage to an almost childlike bewilderment. In his vast experience of fighting he had never met a man like this with no attack. If only he could snatch a rest in his own defence, and let the other fight, he felt that he would sooner or later get the opening he needed.

Instead of which the remorseless steel against him continued to advance with an unbreakable defence. Already they were past the lights, to Doctor Syn's advantage, and the Squire's breathing came in short gasps. Still Syn advanced, pressing his defence upon the elder man. The fumes of wine which had helped the Squire in his first dashes now began to hinder him. His eyes bleared and troubled him as tears of exhausted rage collected in the rims and gave a misty view. Syn's coolness and courage were demoralizing. Apart from that implacable sword advancing so remorselessly, there was that in the parson's eye which drove him back.

"I rather think this is your last fight, sir," said Syn quietly.

How could the fellow fight and talk so calmly? wondered the Squire. The parson's words had pierced his cowardly heart, for he felt a cold sweat of fear flowing from it to his veins. He knew that his strength was snapping beneath the strain. He thought of his loaded pistols in the case. They were far down the room where Cobtree had placed them. In an endeavour to reach them he tried to turn and so reverse positions. This Syn resisted, for he did not mean to lose the advantage of the light. Also he had a wish to drive his opponent's back against the panelling, as his had been. So doggedly, he prevented the Squire from turning, and doggedly he drove him farther up the room.

The Squire's condition was now deplorable. Sweat poured from his forehead, and his eyes were full of tears, so that he had to jerk his head sharply to be rid of them. And so, baffled and weary, he was driven back. At last he touched the panelling, and knowing he was beaten, cried out in a sob of rage, "Will nothing make you fight, man?"

"I rather thought we had been fighting all this while," replied the Doctor.

With his back to the wall, the Squire fought wildly, and with a last despairing effort tried to break through the other's guard.

"Attack him now!" cried Cobtree. "You have him at your mercy."

"Which I will show up to a point," replied Syn, still doggedly defending. "I do not wish to kill him suddenly. His soul is in bad case, and I would give him time to repent upon his death-bed.

Bring me more light here, Tony, and I will do it skilfully." Before Cobtree could pick up one of the heavy candelabras, the Squire, with his last ounce of strength, attacked again. Syn guarded himself with the same persistence he had used throughout, and then, as the wavering candlelight flickered towards them, he suddenly changed his tactics and attacked with the same lightning fury as the Squire had done.

Now, whether what followed happened through a cunning design of the Squire's, who at least knew that he could depend upon the honour of the parson, or from the superior skill of Doctor Syn, but ere Tony could reach them with the lights the Squire's sword shot high over Doctor Syn's head and fell with a clatter on the floor behind him.

"You have him now!" cried Tony.

The Squire crouched panting against the panelling, breathing hard.

Doctor Syn retreated slowly, facing the Squire, until he passed the fallen sword.

Then, with a superb gesture of command, he pointed to it with his own weapon and said, "Pick it up."

"And you'll spit me as I do it," snarled the Squire ungenerously.

"Had that been my way, I could have done it easier three seconds ago," replied the Doctor.

To gain time and recover his gasping breath, the Squire slowly straightened himself, wiped the sweat from his brow, and then advanced towards his sword with weary steps.

"Make haste sir," cried Syn, "lest my patience snap. But I have no interest to kill a man unarmed." Since everyone's eyes were upon him, no one saw or heard the secret panel behind the Squire's back slide open. It was Syn who first saw the farmer standing there. The Squire was about to pick up his sword when the parson said, "For heaven's sake, look behind you!"

"Another trick to catch me unawares?" sneered the Squire.

"I have never tricked you," replied Syn. "I have fought fair. But it seems that other hands than mine must kill you." The Squire realized that all eyes were upon something behind his back, and so he slowly turned.

A bewildered look came over the Squire's face as he tried to recollect where he had seen this man before who now faced him with a levelled pistol in his hand and grim, determined hate upon his face. He was not long in doubt.

"I am Esther Sommers's father," he said, in a hoarse whisper. "I have come to put Paid to your account." A flash, a deafening report, and then, amidst a stench of gunpowder, they saw the Squire's great body crumple down upon the boards. Nothing moved save the twitching of his sword-hand and the curling smoke from the steady barrel of the pistol.

It was a strange voice that brought the onlookers back to a state of reality.

"This looks to me like murder." The speaker, who was quietly closing the door through which he had entered, was richly dressed. He was short in stature, but broad-shouldered and heavily built. His complexion was browned from foreign sun, and his gold earrings indicated the sea as a profession. Unlike the prevailing fashion, he wore his hair short-cropped and his black, pointed beard gave him more the appearance of an Elizabethan than a Georgian. When he smiled, as he was doing then, and showed his fine white teeth, he was not unattractive. About the age of Doctor Syn, he looked older, for he had lived hard and run the pace. His bearing conveyed a recklessness which to feminine eyes at least appeared romantic. Booted and spurred, he carried his riding cloak over his arm, but as he advanced easily into the circle of light he tossed it from him to a distant chair. It was then that Imogene recognized him, for with a cry of joy she sprang forward, seized his hands in hers and said, "Nicholas!"

"Of course," observed Syn to Tony. "It is the Squire's nephew."

"And come in the nick of time to close my uncle's eyes, it seems." His manner was almost jocular as he set the girl aside, with a friendly patting of her hands, and surveyed the dying man upon the floor.

Not even the pains of death which gripped him could disguise the hatred of the Squire as he asked, "Have you come to crow at my death, young cockerel?"

"I hurried from Spain, sir," replied the nephew, "in response to your last letter threatening to cut me off from the estate. I took the precaution of calling upon the family lawyer in London, and no doubt you will be desolated to learn that you have no means of carrying out such a piece of petty spite. He was setting out for Oxford tomorrow in order to inform you of this himself, but, as you see, I have forestalled him with the good news."

"I would have made him find the means," replied the Squire.

"I rather think that the little misfortune which I see you in, dear Uncle, will give me the estate within the hour. I have seen death writ on faces before now."

"Aye, I am done for this time," went on the Squire, speaking with increasing difficulty. "Had I lived tonight, I would have married that girl, whom you had lost to the parson there. I warrant her child would have been a bar to your inheritance."

"What does he mean, Imogene?" asked the nephew.

"It means, Nicholas, that I am betrothed to Doctor Syn," she answered.

"Tonight my mother and myself were brought here forcibly, but Doctor Syn and Mr. Cobtree came to rescue us. Your uncle tried to kill my lover, who proved himself the better swordsman. Indeed, your uncle was disarmed when the shot was fired." Nicholas looked at the man who still held the pistol. "Why, it's Sommers.

You lived across the river. I remember. You had a daughter. I warned my uncle at the time that his peccadilloes would get him into trouble. I think I heard she died."

"Aye," replied Sommers. "He killed her."

"So you kill him," said Nicholas. "Well, all I can say, my friend, is that you are in something of a fix. A duel's a duel, and murder's murder."

"I'll swing for it if needs be. I am glad," replied Sommers.

"Tut, man, let's have no more corpses. While uncle obliges me by dying as quickly as he can, I'll think what's best to do." As a reproof to his callous hatred for his uncle, Doctor Syn took cushions from chairs and propped the dying man into a more comfortable position.

"Leave me alone," said the Squire. "But give me wine." Imogene poured it out and took it to him. He tried to drink, but could not.

Instead he muttered to her through his clenched teeth:

"Will you tell me something, child?"

"What is it?" answered Imogene.

"That fellow Sommers," he went on with an effort. "Regard him well, and tell me how came such an ugly devil to possess so beautiful a daughter. Yes, Sommers, your Esther was a pretty wench. I wonder now if I'll meet the jade?" They were his last words. Doctor Syn knelt by him and felt the heart. Then he slowly rose and said, "He is dead."

"Well, I'll be no hypocrite," said Nicholas. "I always hated him." He picked up the dead man's waistcoat and felt in the pockets. In one of them he found a key, which he carried to a cabinet by the fireplace. This he unlocked and searched amongst the many papers it contained. At last he lit on a document, which he opened in haste. He scanned it through and then said aloud, "To my nephew Nicholas Tappitt, all my estate." Then he looked at the others with a smile and added, "So the rascal did not alter his will. My visit to the lawyer was not true. I said it to frighten him. I think he could have left his money where he would. However, it seems that I am safe. And now, gentlemen, let us see about giving him a more regular death than he enjoyed. I have no wish to see the father of Esther Sommers on the scaffold. If you gentlemen will agree to my plan, there will be no question of murder. At dawn tomorrow Doctor Syn, with Mr. Cobtree here as second, will meet my uncle in an affair of honour. As his nephew I will act for him. I know a surgeon in the town who for a purse of guineas will keep his mouth shut, and certify the death as regular.

We'll play the farce in Magdalen Fields. It would seem a natural meetingplace. No possible blame can fall on Doctor Syn for killing him, unless it is a rap over the knuckles from the University Authorities. What do you say?"

The effrontery of this suggestion seemed to the others so preposterous that they at first emphatically refused. But gradually Nicholas made them see that only by such means could Sommers be saved from trial.

"You may safely leave this to me to carry through," said Nicholas. "All you have to do is escort the ladies back to Oxford, and await me at dawn in the Fields."

"But why in Magdalen Fields?" asked Cobtree. "It could be managed better here."

"The pistol-shots must be heard in a more public place," explained Nicholas. "It will be the publicity of the affair that will deceive. I will bring the body by coach. The surgeon and I will lay it on the sward. Doctor Syn and I will fire the pistols into the air. The corpse will be lifted back into the coach, and Sommers is at liberty to stay in bed if he wishes. As to my servants here, they will obey me implicitly. They ever had a good regard for me, and hated my uncle. Let us release your mother, Imogene, and I will send you by coach back to Oxford." The dominance of Nicholas succeeded, and since nobody had a better plan, they all took an oath of secrecy and agreed to carry out the grim game. Vastly relieved at his salvation and accomplishment, the man Sommers went the way he came, by boat. They found Imogene's mother in sad condition. The terror which she had gone through, added to the physical pains from the brutalities that had been practised on her, had affected her poor brain, and they took her back to White Friars only half conscious. Nicholas, who had locked the door upon his uncle's body, accompanied them in order to arrange with the surgeon, whom he proposed to take back with him to Iffley. The good landlady at White Friars was awaiting news anxiously, and was overjoyed to find the rescue had been accomplished. The three men then left the ladies to her care, and proceeded to the house of the questionable surgeon.

Accustomed to be called out in the night, they found no difficulty in awakening him.

"It is by no means the first time that the rogue has done a dirty piece of work at Iffley," whispered Nicholas as they waited for him to dress. "He'll do whatever I ask of him, for I know enough to get the rascal's name struck off the Rolls." And so it proved. For twenty guineas he promised to arrange things to their liking. He was perfectly willing to accompany Nicholas to Iffley, for he was promised good wine upon arrival, and so they went their way, while Tony went back to Queen's College with Doctor Syn, where they kept vigil waiting for the dawn.

As they watched the night sky, Tony said, "I only hope that the killing of this bully will not ruin your career, Christopher."

"I might have killed him there," said Syn. "At least I have not his blood on my conscience. And I honestly think it would have gone hard with Sommers at a trial. A jury seldom finds a murder justifiable, though this one was, I think. I wonder what the Chancellor's views will be. My good Tony, how glad I shall be when we know the upshot of this somewhat deceitful business!" At the first paling of the sky, the two companions, muffled in heavy cloaks, crossed the Courtyard, and let themselves through the gate with the key which they had borrowed from the porter's lodge some hours before, for Doctor Syn had realized that the rousing of a sleepy porter would occasion noise and attract attention from the students. Once in the street, they walked briskly toward Magdalen.

On the way Tony rallied his friend upon his gloomy countenance:

"At least you are about to fight a duel, with absolute certainty of killing your man, and the finest fighter can hardly say that."

"I only hope this Nicholas Tappitt will not bungle things," replied the Doctor.

"Not he," said Cobtree. "He is as anxious as we are to save this Sommers."

"I have been wondering about his motive," went on Syn. "He did not strike me as a man who would take much risk for another than himself. And I think this plot of his is to insure his own safety. After all, he was in the room when the shot was fired. He was admitted by the servants in the hall. He was known to have a hatred for his uncle, and he had everything to gain by his death. It occurs to me that he does not altogether trust us. Suppose we had chosen to side with the man Sommers, our Nicholas would have been in an ugly case."

"How could we have done that?" cried honest Tony.

"Of course we could have done no such thing, but I think he measured us by his own character."

In this Doctor Syn was right, for despite his easy manner, Nicholas realized that his situation might be dangerous. There were those on his ship now moored in London Docks who knew he had gone in haste to Oxford on a quarrel with his uncle, and where his own safety was concerned he trusted no one. Doctor Syn's cloth, and Cobtree's legal profession, and the fact that both were men of honour, did not weigh with him. He imagined that anybody would commit perjury if it could be safely done. After all, he did not wish his uncle's death to be too questionable, and the duel that he was staging would satisfy the public mind. They would say that Bully Tappitt had reaped what he had sown, and that the noted duellist, who had been a menace too long, had met his just desserts.

Whatever may be said of Nicholas Tappitt—and all through his life bad things were said of him—he did not bungle things. Hardly had Doctor Syn and Cobtree taken their positions by the field gate when they saw the Iffley coach approaching. They opened the gate in readiness, and the coachman drove his team to the centre of the field. The surgeon alighted with his case of instruments, followed by Nicholas with the case of pistols.

Syn and Cobtree went to aid them in the grim task of removing the body from the coach.

"Before we have him out," whispered Nicholas, "it would be as well if one of you gentlemen were to take a look in the ditch yonder. That hedge affords good shelter, and with so many strangers in Oxford for the Fair, it is a likely spot for a homeless tramp to crawl." Doctor Syn immediately hurried to the spot, took a quick look round, and then ran back with the disquieting news that two gipsies were there, one with his head beneath a coat and the other with closed eyes and snoring heavily.

Indeed, as they listened they could her the noise across the meadow.

"If they do not wake before our pistol-shots," whispered Nicholas, "their presence will help us, and the news will fly through Oxford that this affair of honour was conducted regularly. Let us quickly get the body to the grass." After some difficulty they managed to get the stiffened body through the door, and laid it face upwards in the grass. Nicholas dragged away the cloak it had been wrapped in, folded it neatly and put it on the ground. He then brought from the coach his uncle's brocaded coat and waistcoat which the dead man had divested the night before, and had also had the foresight to add a hat to this deception.

"Now, Doctor Syn," he went on, "take this pistol and fire it into the ground when I signal. Measure fifteen paces from the body, and then strip to your shirt.

And now, Mister Surgeon, your bottle."

The surgeon handed a phial containing blood, which Nicholas uncorked and poured upon the dark stain that had congealed upon his uncle's shirt. He then poured a little on the dead man's lips.

"This is my own blood," he whispered to Cobtree with a smile. "I never thought to shed it for my uncle, but wet blood is essential, and the surgeon took it from my arm this last half-hour. Aye, that looks convincing. Now, Mr.

Cobtree, take up your position as your friend's second. We must be quick. It's getting light and those rascals may awake." By this time Doctor Syn had taken his fifteen paces, and had placed his hat and clothes upon the ground.

"Have you seen to the priming of the pistols?" asked Cobtree. "We should look foolish were they to misfire."

"I reloaded them myself," replied Nicholas. "They are splendid weapons and have never been charged more carefully."

Then, after Cobtree had taken his position by the surgeon, and the coachman had driven away to what would appear a safe distance, Nicholas stood above his dead uncle. Since he could still hear the snoring from the ditch, he risked speaking aloud, addressing the corpse at his feet.

"Faith, Uncle, you are living up to your reputation, and are fighting your last duel from the wrong side of the grave." He then nodded to Doctor Syn. The two pistols flashed almost simultaneously, startling the already wakening rooks from the trees above them, and as the frightened gipsies peered over the edge of the ditch they saw the surgeon running with his case of instruments toward the fallen man. They saw Doctor Syn hand his pistol to his second, and as he leisurely put on his clothes he said:

"Ask if the wound is serious, Tony. Also whether he would wish me as a parson to say a prayer."

Tony approached, and the surgeon, looking up, said: "He is dead. But I will extract the bullet while the body's warm. The coroner will need it." It was then that Doctor Syn perceived that they had made an error. The pistol used by Sommers had been a clumsy weapon, and would have fired no doubt a leaden ball of heavier calibre than duelling bullets. He was reckoning without the thoroughness of Nicholas, for, as the gipsies drew near, the surgeon held up in his pincers a silvered bullet wet with blood.

"Lodged in the rib-bone just below the heart," he said.

"Fit it to the barrel, Mr. Cobtree," said Nicholas. "Then we can report to the Coroner that all was regular."

"Aye, it fits," replied Cobtree, marvelling at this piece of ingenuity.

"An affair of honour, eh, gentlemen?" asked one of the gipsies.

"What do you suppose it is if otherwise, you fool," growled Nicholas, making a fine attempt to show frayed nerves. "It is no picnic, certainly. This gentleman is my uncle, and he is dead. Although I acted for him, I will own that he gave the affront and forced the fight. This gentleman who killed him is a parson from Queen's College, and has acted throughout in all honour. The fight was fairly fought. You agree with that of course, Mr. Cobtree?" Tony bowed assent. "And now, you rogues," went on Nicholas to the gipsies, "would a guinea apiece help you to deliver a message correctly? I see you think it would, so here it is. Now go to the Town Hall, and tell the officer in charge that Doctor Syn of Queen's has killed the Squire of Iffley in a duel fought here in Magdalen Fields. And add that the seconds and the surgeon will this morning wait upon the Mayor and give him the circumstances." After making the rogues repeat this message, Nicholas gave them the guinea. The gipsies, however, seemed in no hurry to set out, and as they stared upon the body one of them muttered, "Didn't he bleed?"

Nicholas, who wisely did not wish to move the body beneath their eyes lest the unnatural stiffness of the limbs should seem suspicious, rapped out: "I think I paid you? Go at once." They slunk off towards the gate, where already a few early risers were gathered and watching from the distance.

"The story will be all over Oxford within an hour, and lose nothing in the telling," said Nicholas, with a smile.

He beckoned to the coachman, and directed the vehicle to draw up so that it screened the body from the watchers at the gate. Then they lifted the dead Squire, and placed him inside, drawing the window-curtains close. The surgeon got in to steady the body, and Nicholas turned to the others and said:

"I will see my uncle taken home, and then we will wait upon you gentlemen at Queen's. We can then, Mr. Cobtree, drive to see the Mayor and lay our information." This he said aloud, but as he stepped into the coach, he whispered with a smile: "How beautifully it worked! I can tell Sommers not to fret, I think." He closed the door, and the coach rolled away and through the gates. Syn and Cobtree followed.

"It seems that we must run the gauntlet of a pretty crowd," said Tony.

"Aye," replied Syn, "and where they have sprung from at this early hour, heaven alone knows. The whole business distresses me, Tony. The more so because I have to own to you that I enjoyed that fight last night. Aye, man. I would not have missed a second of the joy of it. Should they unfrock me for this business, I shall leave the pulpit for a more adventurous life."

"You must think the first of Imogene," returned Tony.

"I thought on her with every clash of steel last night," replied the parson.

When they reached the gate, the crowd, which had now so mysteriously increased, held the gate open for them. The men doffed their hats, and such women and girls as were there dropped curtseys. As they passed through the gate, the people raised a cheer. Syn stopped and silenced them:

"I would rather you should weep for the dead than rejoice for me," he said gravely.

"Bully Tappitt was a scoundrel, and deserved to die," cried out one man, bolder than the rest. "It needed a man to kill him and that the man is a parson gives me a better opinion of the Church." At this the crowd cheered the more wildly.

"Come, Tony," whispered Syn, taking his friend's arm and hurrying him along. "Would I were free of this and of the whole damned business." But the crowd were not to be robbed of their triumph against a man they hated. They had most of them witnessed the behaviour of the Iffley Squire in St. Giles' the day before, and to them Doctor Syn was a hero who deserved the fullest acclaim. And so they followed him and cheered him to the gates of Queen's, where their wild enthusiasm roused the porter before

Doctor Syn was able to unlock the gates himself.

"You are a hero, Christopher," said Tony, as they passed the gates. "And you well deserve it for your courage of last night. And remember this. The more popular you are in the public opinion, the more sympathy you will get from the coroner's court, and from the University itself. You may be sure of the students as of the crowds in St. Giles' fair. Yes, I think you will come out of this with honour."

"The whole thing is such a damnable lie," grumbled the Doctor.

"But you have saved Sommers," comforted Tony. "And though you did not actually kill the scoundrel, you might have done twenty times last night. By gad, old friend, I begin to think that your cloth is a mistake. You fight too well to waste such talent. Let us pray that they do unfrock you, and then you can lead a regiment in the wars. Come along; a little breakfast will make you take a more cheerful view of it. I wonder how many innocent lives you have saved from ruin by dealing with this bully. Let that thought comfort you." As they anticipated, the news of Bully Tappitt's death spread like a raging fire through Oxford. That he had fallen in a duel which he had instigated appealed also to everyone's sense of justice. Long before Nicholas Tappitt arrived in his coach to take Cobtree with him to the Mayor, congratulations were pouring in to the young Doctor of Queen's. That the Bully had fallen at the hands of a parson was choice news indeed, and Doctor Syn was accordingly lionized. When at last the Iffley coach approached the College, the way was blocked with carriages and chairs of every description, while the great courtyard and the stairs leading to the Doctor's chambers were filled with the best rank and fashion of the town, all eager and determined to shake the parson's hand and hear the delightful details from his own lips. The unfortunate young Doctor, suffering as he was from lack of sleep and exhaustion, never knew that he had so many friends and admirers. That the parson had won the hand of a rich and beautiful Spanish girl who was visiting the town gave him an additional lustre, since the news had leaked out that this same beauty had been the cause of the duel. The College servants, unable to cope with such a fashionable crowd or deny them entrance, were swept aside, while the fine folk invaded the parson's chamber and fawned upon him through their quizzing-glasses.

The only comfort Doctor Syn derived from all this was the security of public opinion, so that should the Authorities take too stern a view they would be risking their own popularity.

While Tony was wondering how best to effect his meeting with Nicholas Tappitt, since the way was so blocked, he heard that gentleman's voice upon the stairs, boldly announcing himself as "Captain Nicholas Tappitt, nephew and heir to the deceased," and that he had come on urgent business concerning the affair on the authority of the Mayor of Oxford. Knowing the reputation of the Tappitt family, and noting his swaggering demeanour, the dandies of the town made way for him. He pushed his way into Syn's study and bowed low.

"I am come to escort Mr. Cobtree, who acted as your second, sir, in the affair with my unfortunate uncle, to the Town Hall. I have also the honour to bring you a message from the Se—orita Almago, who would be glad to see you at your earliest convenience at White Friars." He then turned to the ladies and gentlemen who had invaded the room. "As friends and admirers of Doctor Syn, ladies and gentlemen, I should like to state most emphatically that although naturally deploring the sudden death of my uncle, for whom I acted in the duel, the behaviour of Doctor Syn has been exemplary throughout. My uncle put such an affront upon him that, in spite of his peaceful cloth, he could not brook. I am about to inform the Mayor that no blame can possibly be attached to Doctor Syn, who fought like a gentleman."

The generosity of this speech did much to put him in the good graces of the assembly, so that when he requested them to leave Doctor Syn to his business, they readily withdrew.

When the door had closed upon them, Syn smiled for the first time that morning.

"Oh, you'll find me well enough yet, I dare swear," he answered easily.

"Come, let us go. We two to the Mayor, and you to the lovely Imogene. By gad, Doctor, you're a lucky man, and I wish you joy. No doubt the little minx has told you that I have been in love with her myself."

"A man of taste could hardly help it, sir," replied the Doctor, as he led them out by a back staircase to avoid the crowds.

This ruse, however, led Doctor Syn into a worse embarrassment, for, a number of his own students spying him, he was lifted on their shoulders and carried to St. Giles' in triumph.

"My little plan has made your friend a hero," said Nicholas as he led Cobtree away.

"I would we were at liberty to praise his swordsmanship, rather than imaginary marksmanship. I shall never see a fight like that again. It was magnificent."

"I can imagine it sir," replied Nicholas. "With all his faults, my uncle was a fighter, and I would have given much to have come earlier on the scene to see him matched." The young men were relieved to find that the Mayor was entirely on the Doctor's side. Indeed, he did not attempt to hide his profound relief that such a menace to the town's peace had died.

They then proceeded to the Chancellor's, who, although applauding his young colleague's courage, took a graver view of the situation.

"Doctor Syn has violated one of the strictest rules of the University," he said.

"But, sir," protested Cobtree, "he went to rescue his betrothed and a man is a man before he is a parson."

"Oh, I know, I know," grumbled the old man. "He was tried beyond bearing, I admit, and a young man of spirit could do little else. But what will our pompous Bishop have to say about the duties of a clergyman?"

"If he unfrocks him," cried Tony, "his Lordship will see his own effigy burned in every quadrangle in Oxford. He had best abide by public opinion."

"Aye, sir," cried Nicholas, backing up the lawyer. "If friend Syn is unfrocked for this, for once you'll see the town boys behind the Gowns, and they'll be for unfrocking every parson in Oxford, the Bishop included." And while his friends were thus arguing in his defence, Doctor Syn, having closed the doors against the boisterous crowds, found peace in his lover's arms.

"I think I am almost afraid of you," she whispered. "I never thought to see a man fight like that. It was horrible and yet magnificent. Promise to keep me always from harm as you did last night."

"Promise to love me always, and I will," he answered fondly.

"I think that should be easy," she replied. "And when my dear mother is recovered from her shock, I am going to make her consent to our immediate marriage. Something tells me that I shall always be in danger away from you.

So let it be soon, and then no separation."

"It cannot be too soon for me," he said.

When Tony and Nicholas returned they had much to tell. That the Mayor and Chancellor were friendly, there was little to fear from the coroner, who would hold his inquiry the next day, and also that Doctor Syn was likely to be called before the Bishop's

Court.

"Suppose they unfrock me, Imogene. Will you still marry me?"

"Oh, if they only would!" she answered. "You are too adventurous for that solemn coat. I'm sure you fight much better than you preach."

"By gad, I think she's right," cried Nicholas.

And Tony echoed, "Yes, by God, I think she is."

"You all seem bent to make a fuss of me," said Syn.

Chapter 7. The Friend of the Family

At the coroner's inquest, held in the card-room at Iffley, it was apparent to the conspirators that no hint of suspicion that a trick had been played upon them had entered the minds of the jury. Indeed, the coroner himself opened the proceedings by stating that the case was a straightforward one, and need not detain them long. In the absence of her mother, who was too ill to attend, Imogene recounted to the court the details of their cruel abduction from White Friars. She stated that while her mother was locked in one room, the deceased had attempted to love her forcibly in the very room in which the court was sitting. She told them of the letter which the Squire had sent to Doctor Syn, and which had been the means leading to their rescue. The unexpected arrival of Captain Nicholas Tappitt, who had known them in Spain, backed by the presence of Doctor Syn and his friend Mr. Cobtree, had insured their safety, but not before the Squire had heaped such insults upon her mother and herself as Doctor Syn, as a man of honour and her betrothed lover, could not tolerate. The result was the meeting next morning in Magdalen Fields.

The three young men were then called, and told the same story. They had agreed that no mention should be made of Sommers or of the secret stairway, but Doctor Syn found himself continually staring at the panel, half expecting the avenging farmer to appear and tell the truth. But having accomplished his work of vengeance, Sommers was wise enough to remain on his side of the river.

After the details of the duel had been given by the seconds, the pistols and fatal bullet were exhibited, and the two gipsies took their stand as witnesses.

The coroner said that there was no doubt in his mind that the duel had been carried out with the strictest regularity between gentlemen in an affair of honour, the jury agreeing that everything was perfectly regular. As a matter of course they were asked to view the body in the shuttered bedroom of the deceased, where the surgeon bewildered their simple minds with the longest medical words at his disposal, and the most of them were thankful that the stiffened dead man's hand was completely covering the actual wound.

A verdict of "Death in an Affair of Honour" was returned, and the coroner wound up proceedings with a tribute to the young parson's courage, and to Captain Tappitt's impartiality. The Captain's behaviour had been gentlemanly throughout, and he hoped he would live long to enjoy his sudden inheritance.

The results of the inquest brought another flood of congratulations to Doctor Syn from all classes of the town and countryside, to which Syn replied wistfully that he had yet to face the Bishop of The Diocese on a charge of violating his cloth.

But the Bishop, neither wishing to fly in the face of public opinion nor to give the appearance that he was swayed by it, pretended to be ill, and begged the Chancellor to take over full responsibility and advise him of the results. The Chancellor pointed out to his Lordship that although nominally Head of the University, and conveniently resident in Oxford, the duty of presiding over such a court must fall upon the Vice-Chancellor, who was responsible for keeping the peace in the colleges. Fortunately for Doctor Syn, this important official was also his good friend, so that when two days later the young Doctor took his stand before an assembly of clergy convened in the Sheldonian Theatre, he felt confident that the court would take no drastic steps against him.

The Hall was packed, not only with students, but with all the fashion of the neighbourhood, and although the Vice-Chancellor thundered against the evil practice of duelling, warning the students that should any of them take part in such an affair he would be sent down in disgrace, yet he owned that in this particular case he felt obliged to deal mercifully with such a brave young man.

Thus was Doctor Syn acquitted, and that very night a supper was given in his honour by the students. Both Tony and Nicholas went with him, and since it was held in an upper room of the old Mitre Inn, the wine that flowed was more than plentiful. In hours of wild enthusiasm, which Doctor Syn was in no mind to check, the jolly students drank themselves beneath the table. Neither Tony nor Nicholas could outdrink Doctor Syn, and they afterwards confessed that although he drank as much as any, he was the only one who remained sober.

Nicholas swore that such a grand capacity was wasted in a parson. But Doctor Syn was yet to know how useful it was to be able to consume more bottles than the next man and yet come out clear-headed.

In the days that followed, Doctor Syn discovered that an

admiration which he had never quite resisted for Nicholas had developed into a fast friendship.

Possessed now of his uncle's wealth, the young man began to enjoy life with zest, and insisted that his friends should do the same and share his fortune with him. Nothing could daunt his kindness and concern, and he would wave aside their continual gratitude with "I am a friend of the family, I hope?" Imogene especially delighted in his company, and Doctor Syn was glad of this, since, owing to the mother's illness, Imogene was kept somewhat a prisoner in White Friars. Nicholas was a welcome relief to the girl from the monotony of nursing.

It was delightful to talk of her beloved Spain to someone who knew it well and could converse in excellent Spanish. He was also a proficient performer on the guitar, and could sing her favourite love-songs.

Seeing that Imogene loved to speak her native tongue and hear it spoken, Doctor Syn resolved to learn, and in this he was helped as much by Nicholas as by Imogene herself. On one occasion when Nicholas had praised him for an improved accent and an ever-growing vocabulary, the Doctor cautioned him in jest with:

"You must take care, you know, for I shall soon be understanding all you say to one another." At which Nicholas laughed and said:

"I have no guilty secret, since I have always told you to your face how much I am in love with Imogene, and one of the things that makes me love her more is that she is in love with one for whom I have the deepest affection. Aye, and for Tony too. He also is a man after my own heart." This affection he took every means to prove, and at this time the lovers owed him much, for when the question of their immediate marriage had been breached, the Se—ora had proved querulous, complaining that her daughter was regarding her as a hampering invalid. This unjust accusation hurt the lovers deeply, but Nicholas, laying the blame upon the mother's nerves rather than any settled wish, at once began to set the matter right, and his business in their affairs had a happy and speedy result; for at his first argument upon the matter, he returned and told his friends that he had persuaded her to admit that she was fond of Christopher, thought him a suitable husband, and that her chief desire was to get well quickly in order that she could take her rightful part in the wedding festivities.

This news delighted Tony as much as the lovers, for it had

been his idea that a double wedding would be the grandest occasion, since his parents treated Doctor Syn as another son. But it was Nicholas who made all the arrangements, and through his energy both sets of banns were cried upon the very next Sunday at Christ Church. The invitations were sent out immediately, and at his own request Nicholas was appointed Best Man in attendance under Doctor Syn.

Some days before the actual ceremony, the Pemburys and the Cobtrees set out with a vast retinue of servants from distant Romney Marsh. All through the preparations Doctor Syn had nothing but admiration for Nicholas, who seemed capable of running everybody's business and his own as well. He it was who even arranged the two honeymoons.

"I suggest," he said, "that Tony and his bride accept my offer of the Iffley Farm in the Cotswolds. The house is comfortable, though remote, and the scenery romantic. They will be well cared for by my tenants. Then, since Sir Charles and Lady Cobtree are to be in London for their annual visit, what better than that you, Christopher, should take Imogene to Dymchurch? You have been offered the Court-House during the family's absence, and Imogene will have opportunity to know the village which will be her future home, when you decide to leave Oxford and become Vicar of the Marsh."

He also undertook to convey the Se—ora back to Spain aboard his tradingship, for the Se—ora had decided to return to her own people after the wedding.

Altogether Nicholas proved himself a "friend of the family" indeed.

Needless to dwell on the gay happiness of those festivities. Thanks to Nicholas, all went with a swing, and when at last the radiant couples drove off in their respective carriages, the many guests declared that never had young married people started out upon the voyage of mutual responsibilities under more favourable auspices. The one tinge of sadness was Imogene's parting from her mother, but it was understood that as soon as times permitted, she and her husband would take passage with Nicholas and visit her.

The days that followed were the happiest of the Doctor's life. He had been granted a month's vacation from his College duties. He was then to return to Oxford work until his induction to the Dymchurch living. Sir Charles had arranged that this should be as soon as possible, since the old Vicar was only too anxious to retire to private life. This kindly old man allowed the young couple free access to their future home, and Doctor Syn was thus enabled to plan the various alterations which Imogene suggested for the house. On the assurance from his uncle, Old Solomon Syn, the Lydd attorney, that there was no great need to study economy, the young parson spent freely, buying whatever furniture and house trimmings pleased his bride. These two rooms were to be thrown into one, to afford the Doctor a more spacious study. This he allowed on her suggestion, on condition that she allowed the breakfast-room to be discarded to give more space to her drawing-room. Each proposal gave birth to a dozen more, until the bewildered old Vicar mildly remarked that they might as well pull the old house down and start to build afresh.

"Oh no!" cried Imogene. "I love these whitewashed walls. They remind me of the white walls of Spain. And if we built another wing to match that of the new kitchens, the old Vicarage would be like an ancient gem in a new setting." And so another wing was planned.

"But what use we shall put the extra rooms to, I cannot imagine."

"I suggest," said the old man—"and hope so too—that ere long you may need nurseries."

"Of course," replied the delighted Imogene, without the vestige of a blush.

"We must have house room for the children, Christopher." Eyeing the back of the house, where the garden ran down in a gentle slope to meet a broad dyke, Imogene clapped her hands as a new idea was born.

"Although I must not disturb you when you work in your library, we would feel nearer to each other if we joined our rooms upon the outside. We could keep our windows wide open and feel we were in the same room."

"Whatever do you mean?" laughed the Doctor.

"Outside our bedroom window," she explained, "we could build a balcony.

Supported by pillars from the garden which we can pave, we would have a lovely Spanish alcove outside our sitting-rooms. In the sun, if it ever shines here, we could sit under it, and when Nicholas comes to visit us he will be able to sing us his lovely Spanish songs. Oh, Christopher, I shall always sit there if you will have it built. You will? You must. To please me?" All this was duly explained to the builder, an old friend of the Syn family and a Dymchurch man, who could build anything from a boat to a castle.

His name was Wright, and he it was who first opened Doctor Syn's eyes to something about his wife which he would never have thought possible.

"I should think well, Reverend Sir," he advised. "These alterations will cost money which will be wasted should your lady wife decide to move. She is no lover of our marsh, I can see."

This attitude had never occurred to Doctor Syn. Loving the Marsh as he did in all weathers, he imagined that others would feel the same appreciation for it.

This worried him, and whenever he saw a sad look come into his bride's face, he wondered whether it was homesickness for Spain and mother, or dislike of the place that was to be her home.

When she realized that he was disappointed at her lack of enthusiasm for the Marsh, she pretended a growing liking for it, but as the time approached for their return to Oxford she could not disguise her joy. He did not know whether this was occasioned by the thought of leaving the Marsh, or the prospect of returning to White Friars, where they had taken rooms. When he asked her outright she gave a different reason. She wanted to be at Oxford to welcome Nicholas on his return from Spain.

"Of course you do," cried Syn cheerfully. "And so do I. I miss the jolly rascal more than I can say."

Chapter 8. The Elopement

Soon after their return to Oxford they received a letter from Nicholas, stating that urgent business had kept him in Spain, and that he had been obliged to let his ship set sail without him, but hoped to be aboard her upon the next home voyage. He asked them to send an answer containing all their news by the hands of his sailing-master, who was then discharging cargo in London Docks.

You will be glad to know, my dear Imogene, that I escorted your dear mother safely to her home, where I have seen her constantly. She is already completely recovered from her shock, and is glad to be once more in the sunniest of countries. I trust, my dear Doctor, you are becoming proficient in the Spanish tongue. It will amuse you to know that I am passing everywhere as Spanish born. This I have done with the Se—ora's connivance, because we found the English are unpopular, owing to the political state of Europe. Will you therefore be so good as to address whatever letters you may care to send to Se—or Nikola Tappittero, which is the high-sounding name I have adopted? You would be shocked to hear how venomously I rave against the British people. It is the only means by which I can get some honest trading. For you, my dear Imogene, I have purchased a scented lace mantilla, if indeed an English parson's wife be allowed to wear such vanity. Also a guitar of such sweet tone that it took my immediate fancy. The case, too, is very cunningly inlaid. For the diversion of our dear Doctor, I have run to earth a fine old edition of comical Don Quevedo. Although no scholar myself, I have yet appreciation for his wit.

Trusting to find you both in Oxford still on my return, I subscribe myself Your Spanish friend of the family, Nikola Tappittero.

A postscript added:

I hope the honeymoons were happy both in Dymchurch and the Cotswolds. I have sent my felicitations to our excellent Tony and his bride.

"Oh, Christopher," cried Imogene, "promise to stay at Oxford till he comes.

Dymchurch seems so far away."

"Are you so anxious for than mantilla and guitar?" he asked, "or is it Nicholas you want to see?"

"I want to be warmed with the reflection of the Spanish sun," she answered.

The mail brought constant news from Dymchurch. Tony and his bride had returned, were duly thrilled at the rebuilding of the Vicarage, which work was going forward rapidly, since the old Vicar had moved into his house at Burmarsh, praising especially the Spanish alcove which they said was something like a cloister. Doctor Syn noticed than Imogene was more interested in this than in all the other additions put together.

"Tony says that the builder has let in two double seats in the wall of it," she said. "He says it will hold us two in one, and them in the other. But when Nicholas is with us with his guitar, I expect he will sprawl all over one of them, just like a lazy Spaniard. But we shall see him first in Oxford. Promise me that, my Christopher?"

"That promise you must get from Nicholas," he answered. "Duty is duty, and Sir Charles is anxious for me to take mine up as soon as possible. My Induction papers will be ready in a week or so, and when I am commanded, I must go. If the house is not quite ready for you, I could come back here to fetch you when it is. I would rather you came with me, though, for we could stay at the Cobtrees', and your wishes for the house could be the easier carried out."

"Let us write and tell Nicholas he must come back on the next homing voyage. He will do it for us." And she made her husband sit down there and then and pen a letter of Spain. To this she put a postscript in Spanish:

You will please be obedient, and not fail us. I cannot leave Oxford without my mantilla and guitar, and my Doctor wants his book. But more than all we want to see and talk with you, Nikola Tappittero of Spain. How I have laughed at that! If you see us before we go to Romney Marsh, you will escape the mists of winter there. Oxford is bad enough. Oh, what a climate! I wonder sometimes how Englishmen are as lively as they are. I hope you will bring us the latest songs of Spain.

Which postscript somewhat distressed the good Doctor. But he said nothing.

After all, Nicholas was no Spaniard.

Though many of the students who visited them were lively enough, Imogene found Oxford people connected with the University took life and themselves very seriously. Even Doctor

Syn, by reason of being the youngest Don, has automatically adopted a gravity of manner suitable to his responsibilities. To Imogene the subjects that he taught were deathly dull: dead languages and Ecclesiastical Law. To cope with such grave writings, he seemed to her to have wrapped his soul in too sombre a cloak. The only thing that he approached with a lightness of spirit was his study of Spanish. Here he was the student and the teacher, and it annoyed her that he did not attach the same importance to her living language as he did to his own dead ones. This fault, although she did not realize it, was largely of her own making, for unconsciously she talked so much of Nicholas and Spain, that in Doctor Syn there began to grow a jealousy. Not owning this even to himself, he gave her no warning that such a thing existed.

During Spanish Lessons she adopted his own manner of teaching. She railed against the smallest mistakes, and pronounced his accent as execrable.

He excused himself by saying: "It is the fault of our cold English voices, my dear. We cannot speak a foreign tongue to the manner born. We are perhaps too aloof to be good imitators. In the colder languages of the North we might become convincing, but French, Italian and your Spanish need a warmer voicing than we can give, and I think no Britisher would ever deceive a native." Her answer irritated him. "Nonsense!" she cried. "Nicholas speaks Spanish like a Spaniard."

"He has lived in Spain," he argued sharply. "And what do we know of his parents? He never speaks of them. If he is fully English, I am much deceived.

Think of his complexion. There is surely foreign blood in such swarthiness."

"If you compare him to your Tony," she replied, "he may not look so English. But why be so ungenerous to your good friend? Is the English complexion the only perfection?" She looked so scornful in the saying it that he took her in his arms and whispered: "Yours is the most perfect complexion in the world. We both agree on that, at least."

"No doubt it will become more English," she answered, "when beaten by those flying mists on Romney Marsh."

"The Southern sun in you will drive our mists away," he said. "And I am sorry if I appeared ill-tempered. I had no right to disparage Nicholas. You have much in common, and for that I like him, and like you to like him. But tell me that you love me?"

"I love you, Christopher." Then she kissed him and smiled. "And might even love you better still, if you would only laugh as much as Nicholas."

"It suits his gay clothes better than my black cloth," he said. "But I'll be livelier when away from all these pompous Colleges. The sooner we leave, the sooner will you see the change in me."

"But you are not leaving till Nicholas comes," she said teasingly. "You have given me your word on that."

"Not that I recollect," he laughed. "But since I can refuse you nothing, there, I promise you. I'll make the rogue my curate, if you like. You could keep him well in order as his Vicar's wife." And at the thought they both laughed and were happy.

To atone for this argument, Doctor Syn constantly talked of Nicholas, expressing hopes for his speedy return, and for the same reason of contrition, Imogene appeared to have lost interest in him.

It had been arranged meantime that Doctor Syn should be inducted into his Living on the day week following the closing of the Oxford Term. As the time approached with no news from Spain, the Doctor became anxious, for he had not calculated that either business or contrary winds could delay Nicholas so long, and he had given his promise to Imogene not to leave, and yet he knew the inconvenience he would cause should he not be in Dymchurch for the Induction. He therefore told Imogene of his anxiety, and found, much to his relief, that she attached small importance to it.

"But you must go, of course, my dear," she said. "We will both go. The Vicarage is finished. There is nothing to delay us. Nicholas must blame himself if he is so tardy. If he wishes to see us at all, he must take the long ride to Kent.

We have at least built a Spanish porch to accommodate him and his guitar."

"You mean that we will go together?" asked Syn, delighted.

"Am I married to you or to Nicholas?" she asked.

"To me, and thank God for it," he exclaimed.

"Then there is no more to be said, but I like you all the more for offering to keep your promise." Battered by heavy seas and hampered by headwinds in the Channel, Nicholas returned to Oxford but two days before Doctor Syn and Imogene were due to set out by coach. Owing to his wife's change of attitude towards Nicholas, Doctor Syn generously welcomed the voyager with more enthusiasm.

"There is no need to inquire after your happiness, Doctor," said Nicholas, "for I never saw you so gay in manner. But what has befallen Imogene? She appears mighty solemn. I trust she is not taking her duties as a parson's wife too seriously."

"She is delighted with your gifts, Nicholas," he answered. "Believe me, she had been most anxious to see you before we had to leave." Seeing that he had now no cause for jealousy, Doctor Syn reproved his wife in private for the cold attitude she was showing toward their friend.

"I am in a mood to be irritated by him," she explained. "He is so vastly pleased with himself. Also I am not feeling very well. I have the heaviest head imaginable, my nerves are all jangled, and with your permission there is nothing I should like more than to spend the day in bed."

Having handed her over to the care of the motherly landlady, who was very fond of her, Doctor Syn was very glad to be able to give Nicholas a solid reason for Imogene's indifference, for he did not like to see such a jolly rogue so dismally cast down. On the advice of the landlady, a physician was summoned, who reported that although there was no cause for alarm, the patient was nevertheless suffering from a nervous disorder and there could be no question of allowing her to undertake the strain of a long coach journey to Kent. On the contrary, he insisted that she must be confined to the house for at least a week.

Doctor Syn, in his anxiety, first thought of cancelling the ceremony of his induction till such time as his wife could recover. In this, however, he was overruled not only by Imogene herself, but also by the landlady, who avowed that the young husband would be better out of the way so that she could give all her care to the patient's recovery.

"There are times," she said, "when a young wife is best left alone in a mother's care. I have had daughters myself, and I know. You may safely leave her to me and the physician, and when your business is done, return to escort her to her new home." Nicholas agreed that the landlady talked sense, and when he had promised that he would ride from Iffley every day to make inquiry, which he would immediately communicate to Dymchurch by stage-coach, the Doctor felt in a happier frame of mind.

"Allow me to know a little more about women than you do, you old anchorite," he laughed. "And since she seems adverse to my presence, I promise you I will not worry her. I will only call her news and submit it on to you."

"I warrant that after a day or so's rest," said Syn, "she will be asking you to sing her your cheerful songs of Spain. I know so well that you will cheer her back to speedy health and good spirits."

"I'll do my best to that end, believe me," said Nicholas heartily. "When you return I will put my best coach and cattle at your command, to make her journey easier." Two days later Doctor Syn knelt by his wife's bed, and with his arms around her took a loving farewell. She clung to him like a frightened child and whispered, "Take care of yourself, dear Christopher, and promise me that nothing shall make you unhappy."

"So long as we love each other, nothing could," he answered.

And so he left her, riding his own house, and leading another which Nicholas had lent him for his saddle-bags.

In this way he accomplished the journey quicker than had he taken coach.

His welcome to Dymchurch was enthusiastic. He found that the builders had competed the improvements to the Vicarage, and he was satisfied that Imogene's every wish had been most tastefully carried out. Joyfully the Doctor wrote to his wife telling her that here was a home of which they could be proud, and in which he knew they would find happiness.

Nicholas was as good as his word, and each day his letters were more cheerful than the last, describing Imogene's improvement. The great day of Induction came, and with great solemnity the Dignitaries of Canterbury instituted and invested their "Well-beloved in Christ, Christopher Syn, Doctor of Divinity, to the Perpetual Vicarage of Dymchurch-under-the-Wall, with all the Rights, Members and Appurtenances thereunto belonging." It was arranged that he should preach his inauguration sermon upon the following Sunday, and then post back to Oxford to bring his wife, whom the whole village were agog to welcome. On the Saturday morning Tony left his friend sitting in the completed Spanish alcove, for the sun was warm and bright, and the Doctor wished to contemplate his address in the open air. He had not been alone, however, above a few moments when Tony returned with a letter in his hand.

"You will forgive me, Christopher, disturbing your meditations, but the Mail has just driven by, and I warrant brings you the most delightful inspiration."

"From our good Nicholas?" asked Syn, joyfully holding out his hand for the letter.

"No, better still," laughed Tony. "It is from Imogene herself. This shows that she is better. I will leave you to read it in peace, and will call for you at dinner-time." For the Doctor was residing at the Court-House.

"It will be nice to read my first letter in her own Spanish garden," said Doctor Syn, smiling happily.

Some two hours later Tony re-entered the Vicarage garden, but this time with his wife upon his arm. Approaching the alcove, the young man called out gaily, "Study hours are over, Christopher. Dinner is served. What news from Imogene?" Receiving no answer, and thinking that the parson might have retired to his new library, they entered the alcove and received a shock. Doctor Syn sat in one of the Spanish seats staring vacantly before him. He sat rigidly, his tightly gripped fists pressed hard upon his knees. All youth had gone from his face, and his cheeks were of a ghastly pallor. His lips were drawn apart in a hideous grin, showing clenched teeth biting hard. But what horrified his friends most was to perceive a vivid white lock that had appeared miraculously in his long raven hair, and, adding to their terror, they both heard a continual deep moaning that steadily arose from his throat.

"In heaven's name what ails you, man?" cried Tony when he could find his voice.

The Doctor's unseeing eyes did not flicker, but the moaning increased until it shaped these words, "The Lord gave, and the Lord has taken away." Without warning the stricken man's finger twitched convulsively, and a crumpled piece of paper fell upon the Spanish paving-stones. Slowly he got to his feet with all the action of an old paralysed man, and raising his arms to the sky, he shook his clawing fingers at what he seemed to see there. He then completed his text with the most damnable alteration, as he cried in a loud voice, full of venom, "Cursed be the name of the Lord!"

"Is Imogene dead?" whispered Tony.

"Had it been only that," he moaned, "you would not have found me here so stricken. I have received a letter straight from Hell. If you have courage, read it." Standing erect, and as tense as a soldier about to be shot, he pointed to the letter, without looking at it. Terrified, Tony's wife bent down, picked it up and gave it all crumpled to her husband, who mechanically smoothed it out, and without knowing what he did, read it aloud in a low, scared voice.

"I cannot ask forgiveness for myself, but just for my mistake. Why did I not guess that I loved Nicholas? He lives in the sun I worship, while you, with all your goodness, float in mists—cold mists. With an aching heart for you and for myself, l must obey the orders of what is stronger than myself. From you I have gone to follow my destiny. You will never find us. I implore you not to seek.

When you read this we shall be far away. We are already fleeing from cold England, and from now the seas will ever roll between us. All blame is mine, not yours. I do not matter. I have damned myself. But I cannot be true to the blackness of your cloth. I could not face a life in Dymchurch mists. The sun has drawn me to him. But that you will serve the solemn God whom you are sworn to serve is the dearest wish of one that was your wife, called Imogene."

Tony crumpled the letter once more as Syn had done, and in a voice choking with tears of rage hissed out, "That spawn of Satan! We'll spit him with good steel like his uncle. This is my quarrel, Christopher. God's curses on them both."

"No, Tony man, I love her!" cried Syn. "I have blasphemed God, but you are my friend." Clasping his hands though in prayer, he hid his face in the folds of Tony's cravat and prayed aloud not to his God, but to his friend. "O spare me a little, that I may recover my strength, before I go hence, and be no more seen."

Following this despairing cry with sobs that shook him to the soul, Nature, or the God whom he had cursed, knowing he could stand no more, touched him with gentle fingers, and snapped all further reason from his brain, so that he collapsed in dead weight against the body of his friend. To Tony, too, Nature or God was kind, and lent him such strength as he had never yet possessed. He lifted the unconscious body of the parson, as easily, as tenderly as he would no doubt carry his own children in the time to come.

Fate, like a dramatist, panders to Effect, but has advantage of the Stage in that many scenes of varying emotions can be played in different places all at once. As Tony laid his friend upon his bed, the treacherous Nicholas was lovingly lifting Imogene over the bulwarks of his ship in London River. And long before the stricken husband woke to face his dismal future, the sails were filled with the winds that were to carry the guilty pair to Spain. As though to hide her shame from the faces of the crew, Imogene took refuge in the cabin.

Sure of her now, and knowing that she could not change her mind, Nicholas left her there. Up in the Round-house with the sailing-master he drank deep.

Towards evening he had to be carried down to the cabin in a drunken stupor.

Disgusted at his condition, and disappointed in herself, Imogene went up on deck.

As the ship swept on through the Strait of Dover, a brisk wind filled the towering canvas, and the full moon showed every detail of the coast. Seeing the girl standing there so long alone, the sailing-master pitied her, and thinking she might take cold, procured a sea-cloak and gently wrapped it round her.

"We shall be altering our tack shortly," he said, "and swinging out into the fairway, so you must take your last glimpse of England, lady. We stand out into deep water to avoid the dangers of Dungeness. We have at least a friendly moon. I never saw the coast so clear. Do you see that stretch of beach inside the Bay?"

She nodded.

"And behind it," he went on, "that long, straight line of bank? Can you see two separate figures? No, there are three. A man and a woman together, and, a little removed, another man? Look through my spy-glass, and you would think that you could speak to them." He adjusted the lens for her, till she said it was clear. "What part of England are we looking at?" she asked.

"They call that long bank Dymchurch Wall," he said.

He heard her gasp, for she had recognized the lonely figure there. Indeed, some half an hour before, Tony and his wife had seen Doctor Syn pass through the Hall door out into the night, and fearing that his dangerous mood might counsel him to desperate ends, they followed at a distance, respecting his solitude, yet fearing its results. He reached the sea-wall first, and stood there watching the white canvas of the full-rigged ship. They did not speak as they approached, but he somehow knew that they were there, for slowly he raised his right arm and with his tapering forefinger pointed to the vessel. Then did the same unspoken sentence echo in their brains. "It is the ship." Ringed in the powerful glass, which brought the spectral figure of her husband close to her, Imogene saw the accusing finger-point. With a strangled cry of anguish, she fell swooning to the deck. The helm swung round upon the altered course. The ship's bell changed, and the sing-song voice of the heaving leadsman on the bowsprit's tackle echoed out, "All's Well." And at the sound the black-robed figure of the parson seemed to grow to an unnatural height, as with his head jerked of a sudden back against the sky, he shrieked out hellish peals of wild, demoniacal laughter. It gave the lie to the "All's Well", and reached the Gates of Heaven with the news that devils still inhabited with the earth.

Chapter 9. The Dead Man

That night Doctor Syn sat in with the Court-House dining-room and drank.

Fearful for his reason, Tony sat with him, faithfully watching, and sensibly arguing. With the trend of his argument was this.

"You are young. Forget all this. You will in time. Stick to your work.

Another happiness will come." To all of which Syn listened patiently, nodding his head in full agreement, and yet with such an engaging smile upon his face that Tony grew with the more frightened.

"I am a dead man, Tony. And being dead, I shall have no fear in dying, and so my adventurings can be as reckless as I will. Cursed of God, and cursing Him, where is there left to fear? Tony, I intend to go to Hell itself, rifle its molten terrors, and pour them into that man's soul. And when he seems to die, his epitaph shall be, 'He feared a man who followed him.'" Doctor Syn finished with the bottle that was before him, and then, getting steadily to his feet, came round with the table calmly and laid his hand with a show of affection upon his friend's shoulder.

"With the heavy hand which God has laid on me shall be light as gossamer to with the weight of terror I shall put upon that man. Aye, 'follow', Tony.

That's with the word. That is my slogan. That is with the key-note of my long revenge. I'll follow him through villages and towns, countries and continents, and through with the watery spaces of uncharted seas. I'll chase him round with the African Good Hope and round with the Southern Horn. I'll swirl down after him in maelstroms and volcanoes. Nowhere shall he crouch for long, but I'll be there and after him. And by with the God whose name I cursed today, I'll get him in with the end. There, Tony, I have had my say, I have sworn my oath.

From now my passion shall be hidden, smouldering in my soul, while outwardly all will seem to be most calm and coldly calculating." To prove these words, he thereupon allowed Tony to lead him to his room.

A few hours later, when Tony, not having slept at all, entered with the breakfast-room, he was astonished to find Doctor Syn

already there, conversing with his usual sense and charm to old Sir
Charles and Lady Cobtree. Tony, whose face showed plainly with
the marks of tragic strain, began to think it must have been a
hideous dream as he listened to with the Doctor outlining with the
trend he was about to take in his sermons that very morning: his
every word and look so proved that he was master of himself. Yet
one thing showed with the tragedy was real. For there, above his
lofty, noble brow, in startling contrast to with the luxuriant raven
hair, they all could see that livid dead-white lock. With the finger
of an Avenging God has set His sigil there, and Tony, reechoing
with the Doctor's dreadful words, "I am a dead man, Tony, and no
one will know," knew for a certainty that all was but too true. He
alone knew, for certainty none did in all that congregation held
spellbound with his oratory.

After his outburst to Tony he spoke to no one of his tragedy,
and no one questioned him. No sympathy was offered by with the
villagers, but they showed their respect for him by holding their
tongues in his presence, and children were cautioned by their
parents against taking notice of that tragic white lock in with the
young Vicar's hair. When with the ordeal of that Sunday's work
was over, Doctor Syn led Tony aside, and said:

"Tomorrow my Odyssey begins, and I should be glad of your
company on its first stage, which I promise you shall be an easy
one. In fact, it is merely a ride to New Romney, for I have need to
visit my Uncle Solomon."

This Tony promised readily.

Chapter 10. The Odyssey Begins

Early next morning with the two friends mounted their horses and rode along with the sea-wall path to with the quaint old town of New Romney.

Not until they reached with the trees that fringe with the outer streets did Doctor Syn break silence:

"I warrant, Tony, that when I asked you to accompany me upon with the first stage of my Odyssey, you made up your mind that it would mean a ride to Oxford."

"I expected you to speak of Oxford, certainly," answered Tony; "and now you mention it, I can speak out the easier. I propose that I shall ride there in your stead. There are certain things to be done there. That villain's pack-horse is still in my father's stables, and should be returned to Iffley. You have many personal possessions left at Queen's, and there is the question of money owing at White Friars. All these things I can settle for you, if you will give me authority."

"To save me pain, you think," he answered. "But there is no more misery in the whole world that can affect me now. Reading her letter, I received my death-blow, and a dead man cannot suffer. No, I must go to Oxford personally, for I have many odd preparations to be made there against my ultimate seafaring."

"You are intending to leave England?" asked Tony sadly. "I feared you would say so."

"But not yet, Tony. No, not yet. Eventually, of course. But there must be no haste. Haste flusters a man, and I have sworn that through it all I shall remain most calm, and most deliberate. That devil, with his damned guitar and Spanish songs, expects me, as a man of spirit, to sweep to my revenge. I shall not sweep to please him, but creep to it. Yes, inch by inch, along the million miles, if needs be. Slowly, calmly and deliberately, but always very surely. I'll play the cat to his pathetic mouse. And when at last he fawns at me to kill, I'll whisper, 'No. Not yet. It is not quite time yet.'" Moved by his friend's emotion, and resenting all that caused it, Tony leant forward, caught his companion's bridle and forced him to the halt.

"Christopher," he said, "if you really wish revenge, leave this affair to me, and you shall have it fully. Suppose I follow them. Kill him, and bring her back to you repentant. Would you forgive her then?"

And at this, Syn laughed, but not unkindly. Gently he released his friend's hand from his bridle, and slowly pressed his horse into a walk, saying through his laughter:

"Oh, my good Tony, you almost persuade me to think that there is a little niceness in this dreadful world. But no, Tony, I have loved as maybe only you could love. But I have lost. And now I chase another mistress, and I find her most alluring. Her name is Revenge." When they reached the old attorney's house, Tony tactfully insisted that he would remain outside and hold the horses.

"I shall not keep you long, I promise you," said Syn. "I have my business at my finger-tips, which will please Uncle Solomon, since I interrupt his working hours."

"You must not hurry on my account," replied Tony. "Besides your business, you will have family affairs to discuss."

"There will be no discussion," returned Syn. "I can tell him the bare facts in a sentence, and then make my business request. A few minutes will suffice for all I have to say." He was as good as his word, for in a few minutes the front door was opened again, not by the man-servant, but by Solomon Syn himself. He saluted Tony cordially, and assisted his nephew in arranging two bulky banker's bags across the saddle.

"Aye, Christopher," said the old man, "they will ride there safe enough, for the webbing is strong, and you know how to tie a knot. If you meet a highwayman, avoid him."

"We should be two to one, Uncle," laughed the Doctor. "We are both armed, and can take care of ourselves, I think." As they rode away he tapped the bags before him and explained:

"Guineas, Tony. I knew my uncle kept a store of them locked in his vault.

On our return to Dymchurch, old Wraight the builder is to meet me at the Vicarage. I wish to settle his account today. It is the first step of my Odyssey.

Each hour I must do something to advance it. I wonder, now, how many years it will take, and how many land and sea miles I shall cover?"

"I still hope," said Tony sadly, "that God will show you there is something better than revenge." But the Doctor shook his head and answered, "There can be nothing better in the world." When they had handed their horses to the Court-House grooms, Tony insisted upon carrying the guinea-bags to the Vicarage, where they found the good old builder awaiting their pleasure.

"There was not this need of hasty payment, sir, as far as I'm concerned," said the old man respectfully.

"I know, but I wish to get it settled," replied Syn. "I see that you have the detailed list of items with you. Give it to Mr. Cobtree to look over, while you and I take a final look at the improvements." So Tony sat down to the library table and checked the inventory, while Wraight followed the Vicar from room to room, and out into the garden, the builder talking proudly of the various results of his work, and the Doctor vouchsafing not a word of comment. Neither praise nor censure did he speak, till his silence worried the old man. Unable to stand it longer, he asked:

"I hope, sir, that my work meets with your approval?"

"Of course. Of course," replied Syn, but in a tone that showed the builder that his mind was elsewhere. "The work has been faithfully carried out, according to my instructions, and whatever mistake has been made, it is mine, and not yours, and I will take the blame."

"Mistake? The blame?" repeated Wraight. "I beg, sir, that you will point out any mistake, that I can rectify it." The Doctor changed the subject suddenly, and pointing to a ladder that leaned against the new wing in which Imogene had planned her nurseries, he asked what it was there for. "I see it gives access to the roof. Is it not finished?" Wraight explained that he had been up there before the Doctor's arrival to inspect the new red tiles.

"Did you find them satisfactory?" asked the Doctor.

"I did, sir. Very pleased with them I was. I wager they'll keep out wind and water for a century."

"I wonder now," said Syn, with a smile.

Bridled that his work should be thus criticized, the old man was angry, but before he could speak, Syn left him abruptly, and walked quickly to a toolshed from which he brought a heavy pick-axe. Then he climbed the ladder and stood upon the gently sloping tiles. Suddenly he laughed, and, to Wraight's astonishment and indignation, he swung the pick above his head and brought the flat blade of it down with a sweeping blow. Using the implement as a lever, he forced the tiles from their pegs and sent them crashing down into the garden below. In a minute he had torn a hole in the roof through which he cast the pick, and with such force that it tore its way with falling plaster into the room below which was to have been the nursery. Dusting his clothes deliberately, he climbed down the ladder and told the amazed Wraight to follow him into the house.

Tony, who had heaped up the requisite pile of guineas on the table, crossed to the window to find out the cause of the noise, but seeing the grim expression upon the two men's faces as they entered, he kept silence and waited for an explanation.

"I have thoroughly satisfied myself, Tony," said the Doctor, "that Mr.

Wraight has carried out the work I gave him faithfully. I see you have the guineas waiting for him, so if you will count it, Mr. Wraight, Mr. Cobtree will give you a receipt to sign. I then shall want from you, my good Wraight, another estimate, which I will pay for now, as soon as we agree. I want all the work which you have executed to be removed as soon as possible. In short, I wish this good Vicarage to be put back exactly as it was. As I told you, I am willing to abide by my mistake, and I do not choose to saddle my successors with so large a house as now it stands. Dilapidations become a heavy charge for outgoing incumbents. You need not question my authority for this, since I have gained the permission of my patron, Sir Charles Cobtree, who, as you know, is warden of this Living. Will you undertake this at once?" Wraight nodded. "It be the strangest job I ever had."

"Ah, Wraight, old friend," said the Doctor sadly, "there are the strangest circumstances connected with it, I assure you, and in giving you this order, I confess I am not thinking only of my successors here."

"We are not wanting your successors, sir," replied Wraight. "As to any other motive you may have, I respect your silence, sir. And in that I know I speak for the whole village, sir."

"God has at least possessed me with many faithful friends," replied the Doctor.

Thus did old Wraight voice for the village their unspoken sympathy.

A few days later Doctor Syn rode back to Oxford. In returning the borrowed pack-horse to Iffley, he found that the estate was up for sale.

So the fox will not return to that hole, he wrote to Tony. He also described the ordeal he undertook while visiting White Friars.

The deeper I plumb the depths of their deception, the higher must I soar in the Heaven of my Vengeance. It appears that the sudden illness of my wife was for the most part feigned. And I dare swear at his suggestion. Hardly had I left her, but he was there and welcomed. He wrote to me each day of her improvement, as you know, and she did improve to him. Why did I not obey a loving instinct that came to me when but a mile outside the town? It was a compelling urge to gallop back and kiss her. Thinking she would be sleeping, I conquered the desire. Had I not done so, I should have found her up and singing with him to those damned guitars. More could I tell you, but why abuse good ink and paper with things so damnable? One fact enraged me at the time, I think almost as much as their worst sinning, for when I asked for my account of accommodation, I found that the rascal had had the impertinence to settle this for me. Since the good lady honestly refused my double payment, I took the amount into St. Giles' and gave it to the first beggar I encountered. My few possessions here I have packed and sent by coach, and I intend to ride back within the next day or so. But I must first glean what information I can concerning our rascal from the servants at Iffley. Disgruntled at their abrupt discharge, they will no doubt be bribable.

On returning to Dymchurch, Doctor Syn continued to reside at the CourtHouse. When the Vicarage had been restored according to his direction, he installed there, at his expense, a married parson, who should act as his curate, and be ready to take over his duties when he was ready to set out upon his vengeance. Tony and his wife, who lived in a separate wing of the CourtHouse, never dared to ask him when this would be, and as the months went by, and still he carried on his work, they hoped he might in time forget. But all the while the Doctor was preparing. Relieved of much of his work, he had ample 238_ _leisure to ride about the countryside. In the town of Sandgate he discovered, to his joy, a Spanish prisoner living on parole. He struck a friendly bargain with this gentleman to teach him Spanish. With him he wrote and read and talked, promising this exile that as soon as he had made him proficient, he in his turn would pay the residue of his ransom and use his influence to get him back to Spain. Many an hour did these two pore over Spanish maps, and from many a lively description Doctor Syn was soon familiar with the manners and customs of that country. Fortunately the Spaniard was well acquainted with the port of San Sebastian, and he described this place so vividly that Doctor Syn could walk the streets of it in imagination. This was important to him, for he knew that San Sebastian was the port of lading for his enemy's ship. The Spaniard was also a master of fence, and knew many tricks that were new to the Doctor, who was able to pass them on to Tony, with whom he exercised with swords daily.

At last there came a day when, in the midst of a lesson, the Spaniard clapped the Doctor on the back and said:

"I have no more need to teach. Your conversation is admirable, and, hardest of all to accomplish, your accent and pronunciation are as good as any Spanish gentleman I know."

"Then I can wind up my business here," replied the Doctor. "I have already settled yours for you, and so the sooner we set sail for San Sebastian, the better we shall both be pleased." It was then arranged that they should sail together, and Captain Esnada—for that was the Spaniard's title—begged of him to stay in his company at his daughter's house upon arrival. Liking him well, and perceiving that he would be of the utmost service to him in Spain, the Doctor readily consented.

It took him but a day or so to arrange with his Uncle Solomon a banker's system by which he could readily draw money abroad, and then, after handing over his full duties to the worthy curate who it was arranged should succeed him, Doctor Syn preached his farewell sermon, took leave of the Cobtrees and the village of Dymchurch, and in company with Esnada took coach to London.

To be sure, he had first taken solemn oath to keep Tony informed of his progress, and as a parting gift bequeathed him his favourite horse, an old and faithful friend he was loth to lose.

"I will but keep him for you against your return," Tony had said. "When you have settled your score, you must return, for you know that my father will see you back again into the Living." But the Doctor shook his head at that. "I fear," he had said, "that my good friend's hunting days will have passed away before I preach again in Dymchurch. In fact, 'tis likely I shall never preach again." This was untrue, as afterwards befell, but it was long years before he was to preach again in Dymchurch.

While waiting for a vessel to convey them to Amsterdam, whence they could re-ship for Spain, Doctor Syn occupied his time in making inquiries concerning the fruit-ship owned by Nicholas. He learnt that it had not returned to London Docks since the voyage of seduction. He was glad of this, knowing that Nicholas was afraid of him. They were not long in Amsterdam, for they found a Spanish merchantman ready to sail the very next day after their arrival, and having no other passengers booked for that voyage, the captain was glad of their company and money.

Now, since they were bound for a Catholic country, Esnada persuaded Syn to drop his title of an English parson, and, as

England was not popular, to confine his talk to Spanish. This the young Doctor agreed to do, and although he still retained his black cloth suit, which was elegantly cut, he changed his white tabs of office for a lace cravat. He had never shaved his head to wear the formal wig then in use for parsons, but wore his own hair long. Also he had buckled on his father's sword, so that on the whole he looked more like a sedate young gentleman of means than a peace-pledged parson. Studious he looked, but resolute. He handled his sword-hilt with confidence, and his manner suggested an alert authority. He was quick to make inquiries from the Captain concerning Nicholas. It happened that the Captain knew him well, and was much amused in telling Syn how that English rascal had adopted Spain in honour of a Spanish girl whom he had recently married.

"And he carried himself wonderfully, like a real Se—or. He is truly Spanish in his talk as you and I, and he boasts of his blood like the most arrogant grandee. He used to make money taking fruit to England when I first knew him, but now he contents himself with carrying all sorts of ladings from one Peninsula port to another. His Spanish wife has cured him of England. 'Tis more than likely we shall meet with him in San Sebastian. You know him, too, perhaps?"

Syn answered that he had the honour, and hoped the meeting would be forthcoming.

On arrival at the harbour, Doctor Syn looked eagerly for his enemy's ship, for there were many of similar rig at anchorage, but he was to be disappointed, for one of the port officials was able to inform them that Nicholas had sailed that morning for Lisbon, but would be returning to San Sebastian with cargo.

The house to which Captain Esnada led him was conveniently placed for Doctor Syn, for it stood up high above the harbour and commanded a fine stretch of sea, so that when out upon the balcony, the Doctor was able, through a powerful telescope, to watch and speculate upon any vessel the moment it topped the horizon.

Finding in Esnada a man of great discretion, Doctor Syn had confided in him something of his purpose, so that the Spaniard, who owed much to the Doctor, was equally anxious to bring the affair to a settling.

"Your Odyssey, as you are pleased to call it," he said, "will be finished shortly. When his ship arrives, we will be standing out there on the harbour wall for his reception."

"Aye, he must come back, as you say," replied Syn; "and yet I have the strongest presentiment that he will somehow give us the slip. No doubt my grim desire to track him round the world from place to place, never letting him settle here or there, has persuaded my instincts to this conclusion. I may be forced to kill him here, and at once; for I fear that my patience would be uncontrolled at first sight of him. Well, we shall soon know." It was one midday, when Doctor Syn was drinking sherry with Esnada and his daughter in their cool upper room, that his eyes strayed back again to the horizon which he always watched. Through the open arches that led to the balcony and showed such a magnificent sea-scape, he had seen a sail appear.

Up she came, a fine and full-rigged ship. In three strides he was at the telescope and swinging it round to bear upon the ship. The unspoken sentence that had stuck in the throat on Dymchurch Wall now passed his lips aloud:

"It is the ship." In a second Esnada was beside him. His daughter, on the other hand, went on reading a broadsheet containing local news, sipping her sherry at the same time. Curious she may have been, and was, if truth were known. But her father, with that tactful courtesy for which the best of his country had ever been famed, had strictly enjoined her never to notice anything queer about their guest. So much did they both owe him for his deliverance from England, that she must never by word or look appear to be sounding the depths of his mystery.

"When I tell you that he has a mystery which is not a mystery to me, I am not boasting of any keen perception, for he did your father the honour of his confidence. Therefore in this house it must be respected, perhaps more than in any other."

Like father, like daughter, she therefore showed not the slightest interest in the ship, at least not outwardly, for this serenely beautiful Spanish lady was middle-aged and very sensible. She had never married because her soldier lover had been killed in war. Grateful to Doctor Syn for having brought here father back to her, she allowed herself a motherly regard for him, and she somewhat envied her father that this attractive but mysterious young man had chosen him instead of her as his confessor.

She heard her father say, as he in his turn looked through the telescope, "You are right, my friend; but it will be a long time yet. Suppose meantime we eat our meal here on the balcony. A soldier's instinct is to snatch what food he can before an action, and we cannot tell when we shall eat again today. At all events, he shall not have the satisfaction of knowing that he has inconvenienced our stomachs."

"Just as you wish, sir," replied Syn calmly. "We can at least watch while we eat. But for my part, the sight of those sails is meat and drink to me." Esnada gave orders to his daughter, who never questioned his reason for thus hastening the meal, and before the incoming ship had grown perceptibly nearer in their eyes, the three of them were served with omelettes, bread and wine.

So obvious was it that their guest was suppressing a growing excitement as the vessel drew slowly nearer, that the daughter thought to put him at his ease by saying:

"Can you wonder that my father used to think lovingly of this balcony when he was in exile? You must own it is a pretty sight. Look at that ship! I have always thought that there is a wealth of drama in a homing voyage. How many hearts are fluttering with excitement like those sails? It is a joyful thing to reach harbour, and home."

"It is indeed," replied Syn, and then he added, with a somewhat grim significance: "Yet, however joyful the anticipation may be, the wise heart should prepare itself against uncertainty. For when you think of it, what terrible surprises, what evil news may not be waiting for someone on that very ship out there? And yet I'll wager that not one of them is contemplating on the possibility of such a shock."

"Perhaps God in His mercy does not wish them to," said the lady.

Their meal finished, and the ship growing nearer, Esnada rose and ordered his daughter to her siesta.

"I'm taking our guest down to the harbour," he added. "The sun will be too hot for you, and our complexions do not matter as yours. But first give me my sword, and our guest's sword too, for there are sometimes worse sharks on those ramparts than in the sea, but the mere wearing of a sword keeps them at a distance."

So armed for battle, the two men left the house.

But Esnada did not go to her siesta. She watched her father and his friend striding away through the idle crowds, many of whom were being drawn by curiosity to see the vessel come to anchorage. But these made way for two gentlemen of such military bearing, especially when they saw the worthy Harbour-master saluting them with the gravest courtesy. Indeed, this official conducted them to the very end of the wall, ordering the loiterers back to a respectful distance, so that the great gentlemen, his friends, might not be incommoded. He then bustled off upon his business.

"There is space enough here for a fight," said Esnada.

Doctor Syn said nothing, but loosened his sword in the scabbard. Amidst the bawling and the singing of the seamen, they heard the orders given for the furling of the sails, as slowly the ship drew nearer to the entrance.

"Will he land hereabouts?" asked Syn.

"Aye," returned Esnada. "The Harbour-master said by those steps there. I could wish now he had not driven away the crowd, for then you could have ambushed amongst them. From the height of his deck, he could spot a mouse upon this quay, and you are so plaguey tall, my friend. Besides, the blackness of your dress against this dazzling whiteness makes you the more conspicuous."

"Oh, I want him to see me," said Syn, with a sardonic smile.

"But he'll skulk then in his cabin, and sent others ashore about his business," argued Esnada.

"If so, and should my patience pass all bearing," returned Syn, "we could find some means of boarding her. No cabin door would keep me out, did I once allow myself to say, 'Now is the time'." Suddenly Esnada heard him draw his breath through his set teeth so sharply that it whistled. Then, without opening his mouth, he spoke through his throat:

"He is there upon the poop. Blue coat, gilt buttons and the white feather in his hat. So he flaunts the badge of his cowardice, it seems. He will do his best to avoid a fight, for there has never been a game-cock yet with a white feather.

You see him?" Esnada nodded: "He is leaning against the bulwark." Instinctively the Spaniard loosened his scabbard, but Syn checked the movement sharply:

"Remember this is my quarrel. You could command anything from me, but not a drop of his blood." He drew a brass spy-glass from his side pocket and brought his enemy the nearer. "This Tappittino, or whatever he calls himself, is a true Tappitt of Iffley, for the rascally fool is as drunk as an owl. If his eyes are not too bleared to see me with, I fancy the sight of me will sober him."

"Do you see a woman standing in the bows?" asked Esnada.

Round swung the spy-glass to the bows. For a few tense seconds Syn said nothing. Then he whispered, "It is she. My wife." Esnada wondered whether his emotion was about to get the better of his friend, for the hands that held the glass began to shake. With the same fear that he might lose his grim determination, Syn snapped the glass into its sockets and thrust it in his coat. Then he said sadly:

"She is far too beautiful to have been spoiled by a devil. I never thought she would be there amongst so many men. Well, perhaps 'tis better I should confront them both." At that instant, Imogene saw him and with a cry of terror raced for the poop, crying aloud to Nicholas.

"He is there!" she cried. "He is waiting there to kill us! Don't you see? The figure in black. The figure in black. It is my husband—Christopher. I tell you it is Doctor Syn."

Frightened by the vehemence of her terror, Nicholas jerked himself into soberness. A cold panic drove the drink right out of him, as beads of perspiration burst from every pore. With clenched fists she beat against him like a terrified child. She drove him into instant action, for springing at his sailing-master he cried out with an oath to "'Bout ship!" Ignorant of what dreadful catastrophe was about to fall upon them, their panic impelled the crew into a quick and blind obedience. The sharp and ringing orders were promptly answered, and the ship, dangerously swinging round in a water-space that was hardly adequate, all but crashed into the masonry of the quay. As it was, the helmsman's skillful steering did not avoid a staggering scraping from the wall.

"What are they doing? Good God! are they mad?" cried out the Harbourmaster, and his question was echoed from the crowd.

That there was method in their madness became at once apparent, and with sails already unfurled again she was standing far away to sea.

The Harbour-master came puffing up to the end of the jetty and, making a funnel with his hands, bawled out, "Santa Maria, what is wrong?" But since no one on board the Santa Maria called back, Doctor Syn vouchsafed a suggestion:

"It almost seems as though they had seen some dreadful phantom who frightened them away."

"I never saw a ship do that before," replied the Harbour-master. "Right to the mouth of Port, her cargoes eagerly waited for, then of a sudden, round, at great risk to the ship and all upon her, and off to sea. Look, she is sailing resolutely, as though all Hell were after her. I think, good Se—or, you are in the right of it and this is devil's business."

As he hurried away to write down in his harbour log of the extraordinary occurrence, Doctor Syn turned to Esnada and smiled. But the smile was very grim.

"I am glad there was no kill today, for I think this is the method of torture to employ. He was obviously afraid. The poor, sly fox! Well, I have covered his cover at Iffley, and I've covered his cover here. He will not dare to go on breaking harbourage like this. He must put into some port, and from that port he must sail. We must get a system of spying on him, my good Esnada, and make it so perfect that should we miss him at one port, we must find whither he has sailed, and post by road or faster vessel to arrive there first." With the help of the Harbour-master, Esnada was enabled to get in touch with agents in the different ports of the Peninsula, so that in a little the movements of the Santa Maria were known to Syn before she made them. No sooner was her destination known, but the Doctor would set off to await his arrival. But Nicholas was cautious. He was also very much afraid. The certainty of seeing that mysterious elegant figure in black for ever standing before him upon the end of every harbourage he sought got on his nerves. As he could not run away each time, as he had done at San Sebastian, he would never anchor save in mid-water. He set a guard to watch his enemy continually, with the strictest orders that on no account was he to be allowed to board the ship.

Nicholas himself could never go ashore, for even in the dead of night, although the figure of Syn might disappear for an hour or so, he knew that it would reappear again without a warning. And, as Syn guessed, Imogene was just as frightened as Nicholas, and their horror communicated itself to the crew, who, whenever they landed either on pleasure bent or for business connected with the ship, avoided contact with the figure, never lingering in case it might address them. The mere fact that it never seemed to notice them filled these fellows with superstitious dread, and the hardest dogs amongst them would cross themselves devoutly as they hurried by.

And this went on and on, until the Santa Maria disappeared. She was due to arrive at her port of lading, and, as usual, Syn was there. But this time he waited in vain. He then travelled back the longest road through Spain right from Cadiz, the port in question, to rejoin Esnada in the north. There, month after month went by, and to all inquiries the various agents' answer was: "No news of the Santa Maria." After a year the agents answered finally, "She is posted amongst the Lost." But this Syn resolutely refused to believe. He told Esnada that is was only a question of waiting, and that sooner or later he would surely hit upon some clue as to the whereabouts of his enemy.

In the meantime Syn set himself to study languages. He added Portuguese to his Spanish, and polished up his French.

"And I shall add to these as time allows," he said, "for wherever the rascal may have hidden, when I shall reappear to him it will be useful if I can speak the language." Esnada and his daughter humoured him, but they were glad of the way things had befallen, for they were fond of the Doctor, and had missed him badly when he had been travelling from port to port. And then at last news came.

It was the Harbour-master who brought it in the shape of a sailor. A native of San Sebastian, he had just returned home from the Americas. He had been a member of the Santa Maria's crew for a long time, but had left her in Charleston when she was put up for sale. The owners had bought a shallower craft to trade up-river.

Oh yes, indeed, the owner's wife was with him. She had a child, too—a boy —and by this time doubtless had another. The husband, Black Nick, was for ever dragging her around with him, baby or no. The sailor went on to speak of Black Nick's bad habits: drinking and the worst brutality. When Syn gave him three guineas for his story, he was back again next day, with details he had not thought on.

Esnada warned the Doctor not to pay more heed or money, for he thought the rascal had realized that they had no good regard for his Black Nick, and so, by further blackening his character, he thought to purse more guineas.

"Besides," he added, "'tis months and months since he set eyes on your enemy, who may be anywhere by now." This did little good in swerving Doctor Syn. He was determined to follow his destiny, and that was clearly pointing to America.

"It is so vast a continent," objected Esnada.

"All the more room to follow him about in," laughed Syn. "And 'tis something to know what continent he is in." A few days later, writing to Tony Cobtree on the subject, he ended with:

"And so I go to America. It is the only thing I can do. Perhaps I am called to convert the Red Indians—who knows? Or perhaps they will convert me.

Well, I know whose scalp I hunt. Life in England, despite your father's entreaties couched with yours and your dear wife's, I fear, would be to me unbearable at present. It may be long before I see you, but I cannot think that I have walked my last on Dymchurch Wall."

A month later, having taken a sorrowful farewell of his

Spanish friends, he crossed into Portugal and sailed from Lisbon on the Intention, a cargo vessel bound for the port of Boston in Massachusetts.

Chapter 11. Pirates

The Intention was not a fast-sailing ship, but Syn was in no haste. It pleased him to think that his following would be slow but relentless. Yes, dead slow if needs be, but always deathly sure. It was this that counteracted his boredom of that ship for the company was not congenial to a man of his parts.

The Captain, a New Englander, was the poorest sort of man, maudlin in his cups, and miserable out of them. Religious, too, according to his lights, which taught him that when anything went wrong and usually by his own incompetence, all he had to say was, "It is the Lord's Will," and the blame was shifted to the Deity. Certainly his gloom of manner did not cheer the spirits of those beneath his charge.

Officer and men were a mixed set, for, since his original American crew had deserted rather than make the return trip upon such a ship, which they condemned as unseaworthy, and the Captain to perdition, the very sweepings of the slums had been pressed into service. Mostly Portuguese, they quarrelled incessantly amongst themselves, and showed no respect for their officers.

Besides Syn, the other passengers, six in all, were disappointed merchants from Lisbon, who were going out to found a colony. At least, that was what they boasted. But they argued so much about this and that connected with it, and so persistently quarrelled for the post of being the first Governor, that Syn advised them to conquer themselves before attempting to conquer territory. What would have happened had they ever founded that colony will never be known. The obvious conclusion is that their scalps would speedily have adorned the belts of war-like Redskins. Instead their fate was just as terrible, for they were destined to walk the plank.

It was in mid ocean that they fell in with the pirates, and early one morning, under a bright sun shining upon a tranquil sea. The Portuguese passengers had been grumbling at the slowness of the vessel, but the Captain argued that the best navigator could not make pace without a wind. It was then that the topsails of another vessel appeared over the horizon, and Syn, having watched her for some time, remarked dryly that there seemed to be plenty of breeze yonder. The ship was indeed fast overhauling the Intention, and heading, too, in their direction. After the weary weeks on a slow ship, and an empty ocean, this sight of another vessel cheered the company. But even then, speculations as to what she might be became cantankerous. One thought her Spanish, another Dutch, and so on. Doctor Syn settled this argument by the help of his powerful spyglass.

"They fly the English flag," he said.

"I hoped she was Portuguese," said one of the passengers.

"There are worse colours than the English," snapped the Captain.

The vessel came on a spanking pace, throwing white water briskly from her bows.

"They know how to handle her," said Syn.

Quick to take offence where none was meant, the irritable Captain cried, "How can I handle the Intention? I told the owners she was overdue for careening, but they would not spare me the time. Do you hear a creaking?"

"Aye," replied Syn. "It is the mainmast. She is sprung."

"I told you that," retorted the Captain. "But I think otherwise. It is the barnacles that are so clustered on her keel that they scrape the floor of the Atlantic."

Syn laughed good-humouredly and said, "No doubt we shall reach our port in time, for the barnacles can carry us." Meanwhile the other vessel, which was the more plainly seen by all on board with every tack, showed heavy guns from all her hatchtraps.

Asked what she was, the Captain told the Portuguese that she must be one of England's finest fighting ships, and no doubt was carrying some important personage to the Colonies.

"Hardly that, I think," replied Syn. "She is well handled, true, but not in the manner of the Royal Navy. Her officers alone would tell me that. The men, too, are as rascally as ever I saw on shipboard."

"But they employ the roughest dogs in the English Navy," sneered a Portuguese.

"But, sir," retorted Syn, "there are indeed worse flags to be met at sea, as the Captain said, than the English colours, and, by gad, they're going to run up the blackest." To the horror of the Portuguese, the English flag, which for all their sneering had lent to them a feeling of security, was being struck, and in its stead up went the dreaded Jolly Roger.

"The Skull and Cross Bones!" cried the Captain.

"Pirates!" cried the passengers.

"Pirates!" re-echoed the crew, with equal fear.

"It seems, gentlemen," remarked Doctor Syn calmly, "that we are faced with a fight, and by the look of it, our adversaries appear to have advantages." He turned to the Captain briskly, and said, "I'm sure I speak for the rest of the passengers. We are under your orders, sir, and will fight as you direct. Thank God we have no women or children aboard."

But his gallant bearing had no effect upon his companions, who were terrified. Indeed, it was the Captain himself who ran to the cords and hauled down the colours.

"We can only treat with them so, and plead for our lives," he whispered.

"Faith, sir," cried Syn, "I hardly think they'll consider some of them worth the sparing."

"They will be short of hands," said the Captain, trying to raise his own spirit. "For my part I shall not be the last to turn pirate. We only live once."

"I thought you were religious," said Syn, "and I hoped to hear you say, 'It is the Lord's Will'. Also I fear your hopes of being recruited are in vain. They do not seem so short of hands." Indeed, as the black flag had been run up with a cheer, the roughest villains swarmed from hiding all over the decks. A shot was fired, which struck with perfect marksmanship, bringing the sprung mast with a hideous crash upon the deck, killing outright a member of the crew.

Then, on that quiet morning sea, a pandemonium arose. Boats were lowered, and in a few minutes the deck of the Intention was alive with the rascals. They were led by a gigantic negro, gaudily dressed, who cried out that his name was Black Satan and that he was Captain of the good ship Pit of Sulphur. This was true, for Syn, who stood apart from his cringing companions upon the poop-deck, had read this ridiculous name enscrolled around the pirate prow.

"Come down and do homage, you lost souls," cried Black Satan from the well-deck.

Led by the craven New Englander, the Portuguese obeyed promptly, and knelt before the great negro abjectly, while he kept whistling a naked cutlass over their heads, and progging their flesh with its point.

"I am the Captain of this ship," faltered the New Englander. "I am the best seaman and can navigate. I will join the Brotherhood." Captain Satan (for he was indeed the Captain, and notorious too as the only negro who had commanded whites on the high seas) now spat in his prisoner's face.

"You navigate?" he roared. "I never saw such handling of a ship. Take him below, my bullies, and see that he shows you the ship's treasures. And you others, run out the black plank. The funeral plank, my lubbers. We provide it for you as your undertakers. Empty their pockets, then let 'em walk. Tie up their eyes with their own kerchiefs." Then, amidst the lively cheers of the pirates, a gangway was opened, and a black plank which they had brought for the purpose was run out over the water.

"Spare us," cried the wretches. "In the name of the saints."

"Talk not of saints to Satan," cried the negro. "Along the bridge, you dogs, and down. The bridge that leads to hell." Blindfolded and pricked with cutlasses, they were hustled one by one along that quaking, springy bridge. Steered by cold steel on either side, most of them reached the end, stepped into air and fell into the sea.

"Swim to the other ship," cried the Negro, shooting down any who clung to the hull of the Intention.

Those who could swim attempted this, but when half-way across both ships used them as targets for not only pistols, but cannon. By this time the craven Captain was brought back from below, behind a procession of robbers heavily laden with sea-chests, bales, barrels and casks, which were quickly lowered to the boats and carried to the pirate ship. Now, it so happened that amongst those chests was Doctor Syn's, and he watched it being lowered as he leaned over the bulwarks of the poop.

"Careful with that, you dogs," he cried in Spanish. "It is of the utmost value to me, I assure you. So see to it that I find it safe when I come over with your Captain." Thinking that he must be a grandee who had saved his life by offering sufficient ransom to Black Satan, the Spaniards in the boat called back, "Si, Se—or." Now, so engrossed were the others at their hellish work that no one noted Doctor Syn, or, if they did, perhaps they did not relish closer quarters with his long steel. By this time the whimpering captain of the ill-fated Intention was dragged towards the plank.

"But I can navigate," he pleaded.

"Then navigate yourself along that plank," snarled the negro.

"I will do anything to please you. I will be your slave in all things only spare my life."

Prodded without mercy to the end, he turned and made a last appeal.

As he stood there abjectly pleading to a nigger, Doctor Syn's gorge rose, and when a facetious pirate shook the plank and the victim fell on hands and legs astride the plank like a child on a rocking-horse, he drew one of his pistols from his sash and wondered how long he should allow a white man to demean himself before a nigger. A captain of a ship should face death bravely. This was too undignified, and Syn vowed it should not last.

The captain had not been blindfolded, and tears of self-pity and terror rained down his cheeks. Syn took careful aim and fired. The body crumpled and slipped from the plank into the sea.

"And who the devil are you to put him out of his misery without my word of command?" demanded the astonished Satan, seeing Syn for the first time.

"Come down here, you dog."

"Better not call me a dog," replied Syn, with a smile. "I once had a dog that killed blackbeetles. As to putting that man out of his misery, I intended no such thing. I shot him because I hate a coward, and especially a white coward who can cringe to a nigger, and more than all a cowardly captain who betrays his ship in the hopes of saving himself. You are a captain, too, you say, though I can hardly think that some of these white men fighting for you would not make a change. The question is, Mr. Satan, if that's your name, are you a cowardly captain? That I intend to prove." With a bellow of rage Black Satan leapt for the poop companion stairs, swinging his cutlass. What was his astonishment, however, when he found a calm and elegant gentleman waiting for him with a thin blade, which somehow all his lashings could not pass.

"Get down upon that deck, for I have a mind to drive you out upon your plank. You won't? Oh yes, you will. Down with you, nigger."

Chapter 12. Syn Buys a Body and Soul

Down on the well-deck they fought; and an ill-matched fight it was. A giant of a negro with a heavy cutlass which he swung murderously, but with little skill, against a lithe parson whose thin point of steel kept the scythelike blade confronting him doing nothing but slashing the air, so that although the negro tried to attack and carry it by sheer weight, the needle-point of Syn's sword drove him back step by step. When they perceived that the negro's strength was of no avail, Syn heard the pirates arguing whether or no they ought to interfere. The most of them were for keeping to Brotherhood rules, which state that a fight between two antagonists must be fought fairly, but to the death. One rascal, disagreeing, tried to trip up Syn as he advanced. Syn turned like lightning; passed his sword through the man's neck, and drew it back just in time to meet the negro's next charge. He more than expected that they would rush him for this, but was relieved to hear several cry out that it served the fellow right, and so the wretched man was left to bleed away his life upon the deck.

After this incident, Syn resolved to keep such favour as he had gained by quick action, and to terminate the fight spectacularly upon the plank itself. So, feigning to be weary of such a clumsy swordsman as the negro captain, he redoubled the speed of his lunges, and every time he let the blade prick the flesh, driving his man before him to the plank. Each time the tongue of his sword bit flesh the negro slashed at it in rage, and with such force that one blow might well have broken the more fragile weapon. But Syn avoided every stroke with ease, and still drove the maddened captain back. At last the gangway was behind him.

"A little to your left, now," said Syn calmly. "Feel backwards with your heel. Excellent fellow! Do you feel the plank? That's right. Well, you go along it backwards, for I have a mind to fight you upon it. You will at least afford a novel entertainment to your jolly dogs." And so, inch by inch, he pressed him out, till both were on the plank, cautiously balancing as they fought.

"Steady," warned Syn. "If you wobble like that you will be overboard, and we shall have to finish our fight in the water. And, my faith, that is a good idea.

A sword-fight in the sea is something new. Hold your cutlass tightly. Back, back, back."

Doctor Syn, to show the pirates the light regard he held for danger, then began to sing, and the words he used were those which had come into his brain so long ago in Romney Marsh.

"Oh, here's to the feet what have walked the plank!"

The negro, still driven back, could no longer swing his cutlass for fear of falling from the plank. Instead he tried to take a lesson in fencing from his opponent, and use the point. But though he had a long reach, it was of no avail, by reason of the dancing, darting blade of Syn.

And then the negro felt the point pressing his breast-bones. His heels were already on the edge of the plank. Quickly he turned, and jumped. Prepared in time, Syn kept his balance wonderfully, till the board ceased to vibrate. Then, quite calmly, he stopped, still balancing cautiously, took off his buckled shoes, and threw them on deck. He then peeled off his coat, rolled it into a bundle and shot it after the shoes. His scabbard and pistols followed, which he saw the pirates scramble for as he loosened his cravat. As he did so, he noted that the dying man upon the deck was drinking from a rum bottle, but at that moment his eyes glazed and his teeth bit through the neck. This incident, and the fact that he had seen numerous corpses floating between the two vessels, gave him the inspiration for the rest of his chanty, and rolling up his sleeves he sang:

"Oh, here's to the feet what have walked the plank, Yo-ho for the dead man's throttle.

And here's to the corpses afloat in the tank, And the dead man's teeth in the bottle!"

Then, without waiting to see what effect it had upon the pirates, he used the plank as a diving-board, running along it, and with a crashing spring upon the end dived head foremost into the sea, his sword straight before him. He came up almost as soon as his head was under water, and with blade extended like a swordfish, he glided rapidly through the water with a strong one-arm stroke.

The negro, well used to water, was yet a slow, clumsy swimmer, so that Syn was able to gain upon him rapidly, and it was but halfway between the two vessels when the negro felt the prick of Syn's blade upon his shoulder, challenging him to turn and fight. In desperation he turned, trod water, and slashed with his heavy weapon, hoping to beat the long blade from Syn's grasp.

Then followed the strangest duel that could be fought. Borne on the gentle swell, one higher now, one lower, up and down in turn, they thrust and splashed—the negro desperately slashing, sinking, spluttering, but always rising to a fresh attack; Syn, calm, but quickly pricking when the negro came too near.

Suddenly Syn was aware that a pirate from the Sulphur Pit was jumping from the bulwarks to the rescue of his captain. With a long knife in his teeth, he swam rapidly towards them. Syn knew that the two would be too much for him, and that he must kill the negro first. Aware of help at hand, Black Satan turned, swimming in a half-circle, to put his adversary between them. It was then that a cry of horror was raised from the pirates on both ships, for the great fin of a man-eating shark, attracted by the unusual feast of corpses already awaiting him between the vessels, came skimming towards the two combatants. Syn, knowing that the other pirate was striking out rapidly behind him, seized the crest of the swell and with a tremendous effort drove his sword out and head down-wave, straight at the negro below him. There was a spurt of blood discolouring the water, and then the swell rose again, with the negro this time on its crest, but pierced through the heart by Syn's long blade. Syn wrenched to free it, in order to turn and do fresh battle with the other pirate. But as the body of the negro sank, the blade was wedged, and just as Syn was about to leave in order not to be dragged down, the legitimate pirate of the seas swept towards and at him, in a streak of white foam. He saw the black back turn as the creature dived, and the flash of the white belly beneath him. The great jaws opened and snapped. He felt a mighty pull upon his sword, and then he was free, with the weapon still in his hand, while a track of reddened water shot away some thirty yards to end in a churning maelstrom as the shark sank with his prize.

One of his enemies disposed of, Syn now turned to face the other, the pirate with the knife between his teeth. He vowed that he would at least get him before it was his turn to fall a victim to the shark. He rose on the swell and looked around. There seemed to be no other fin in sight. The huge wolf of the sea that had so obligingly freed his sword for him was no doubt a lone-hunting shark. But the human shark with the knife between his teeth was near at hand, swimming at him and unafraid of sharks. Syn trod water and awaited him.

"Come on," he cried. "This is a new sport: spitting pirates and feeding sharks by hand and skewer." His new opponent came nearer with a grin. He then trod water like Syn, and taking the long knife from his teeth said pleasantly, "Good morning." Syn laughed aloud. The situation was incongruous, and the remark so out of place despite the lovely day about them. He liked the rascal's sense of humour.

"Aye, it's a grand morning for a fight," he laughed, wondering whether the fellow would dive beneath him and stab up, or risk all with a fling.

But the pirate seemed in no hurry to do anything but smile, till Syn demanded:

"Are we waiting for the shark to return with an appetite, or are we fighting?"

"I have a score to settle with you," replied the pirate.

"For killing that damned nigger?" asked Syn. "How could you as a white man have brought yourself so low as to serve under such a man?"

"Black Satan had his qualities, as you might say," returned the pirate.

"Useful enough at terrifying peaceful folk and getting at their treasure. But he wouldn't have lasted very long. I had already planned a mutiny against him, and 'tis like as not that had you not killed him for me I should have done so myself. But now as to our score. It's a long cry from here to Romney Marsh, and I owes you a little matter of three spade guineas, two crowns and a silver fourpenny. And for that sum of money, which helped me on my way to Portsmouth safe from the ruddy Customs, I promised that if you gave up the pulpit, Doctor Syn, went a-voyaging, and fell into my hands, you should not walk the plank but the poop-deck, with a sword at your side and a sashful of pistols. And here it seems we be, just as we thought might happen."

"By gad it's Mipps!" cried Syn. "The little smuggler on Lympne Hill."

"Quite right, sir, and very pleased to meet a Syn o' Lydd this nice bright morning in mid-ocean. Give us your hand, sir, and how d'ye do, and let's get back to the ship and have a brandy before the old shark comes back and interferes." It was then that the pirates saw a strange sight, for the swimmers, changing their weapons to their left hands, shook hands together so violently with their right that the water splashed and splashed again. Then side by side they swam towards the pirate ship, Mipps bawling out to his men to stand by the rope ladder for "two ruddy Admirals comin' aboard." They climbed the ladder none too soon, for the shark was back again in the fairway between the two vessels, tearing at one of the corpses that had walked the plank. But Mipps cared nothing for sharks. He was bent on getting a favourite reception for his one time patron with the pirate crew. He climbed up first, whispering to Syn to follow, and to take his lead in all he said.

"Black Satan's dead, my lads," he cried out, as soon as he had helped Syn to the deck. "And it is my gallant friend here who has saved us from what would have been a bloody mutiny. We all agreed as how the nigger had been over-areachin' of hisself of late; and why should men of brains serve under what was only brawn and muscle? Now, I can vouch right here and now for this man.

You've seen him fight. You've seen him give Black Satan to that ruddy shark.

And did it very neat, you'll allow. His name is Syn, and Syn's as good a name as Satan. Now, I propose we celebrates our victory over the ship yonder in the usual way. Double rum for all hands. Then we'll divide the plunder into portions as agreed and split Black Satan's share. But let me tell you this. We ain't got a more valuable bit of plunder off that there ship than this 'ere man.

Used to be a parson till he couldn't stomach it no more, and so come out here to find me and the way to go a-pirating. I owes him my life for saving me from the Customs officers who was about to hang me, till he steps in and knocks 'em all to hell, parson though he was. I now advises you one and all to shake hands on his friendship, for if you don't, God help you. He's willing to join us, and when you know him better you'll say we're lucky to get him. So serve the grog, then for the plunder, then we'll decide the fate of the ship yonder and also vote a new leader in Black Satan's place."

"Faith, the sooner you serve me with rum," said Doctor Syn, "the sooner will I be pleased. When I have drunk, I am willing to fight my way into your good graces. I will take on any challenger just to prove my mettle. You do not know me, but I am hoping we may be better acquainted either with this" (holding out his right hand, and then putting his sword from his left into it, he added) "or this. But first a bottle of rum to get the stench of that damned shark out of my innards."

The quartermaster produced two bottles, one of which he handed to Mipps and the other to Syn, saying, "You've earned your drink this morning. But have a care. 'Tis strong stuff for a parson." Syn laughed somewhat scornfully, drew the cork with his teeth, spat the cork on to the deck, and then tilted the raw spirit down his throat till the bottle was empty. Mipps was still drinking his, but had only got halfway when Syn took it from him in the most engaging manner and finished it for him. This touch of comedy appealed to the pirates even more than the tragic splendour of his fighting, and in a few minutes, when the grog went round, the pirates were drinking to their new brother's health. Fortunately for Syn the crew was widely recruited from many lands and languages, and when they found this uncanny stranger could speak and joke with them each in his own tongue, their admiration knew no bounds.

"I said we'd strut the poop-deck," whispered Mipps, "and it looks as though you'll be made captain willynilly." And Mipps was in the right of it too, for after the Intention had been abandoned and sunk, votes were taken for the post of command and it was Mipps and Syn who carried it.

It was not till after sunset that Syn was able to take Mipps into his confidence, for till that time they had not been alone. They now found themselves in possession of the captain's cabin under the poop. The pirates had unanimously agreed that theirs should be a joint leadership, Mipps maintaining his post as sailing-master and navigator, and Syn to be in command of fighting tactics. In this capacity he quickly proved himself a leader, for he called for a full inventory of arms aboard, and was much surprised to learn that there was no such thing.

"Then the sooner I have it the better," he had cried. "That Black Satan of yours may have left all to chance, but if I'm to be of use to you my way is different. How can I judge whether to risk your lives and such booty as you already possess unless I know to a nicety what powder and shot I have in the lockers? I suggest that you appoint for us a Master Armourer with sufficient men to help him, who shall be free from all other duties. Not only will they keep our guns sweet and clean, but it shall be their responsibility to keep a razor edge on all your cutlasses. Each day you will choose two of your fellows to come with me on my inspection, so that you will feel satisfied that all is being done for your profit. If we are ready to fight upon an empty sea, we shall be the better prepared when any sail tops the horizon. We must school ourselves to think that we are not here for the fun of the thing. Plenty of time for fun when we go ashore and spend our money freely. But to get sufficient money we must work. If I am to take a hand in leading you, it shall be my object to stuff your belts with guineas and to keep your bodies from the chains.

I take it that none of you desires to hang, and for myself, I don't intend to, for 'tis a most ungentlemanly end. To avoid this, I tell you now there must be no foolishness. Certain risks I am willing to take if I think the possible results are justifiable, in which cases I shall be the first to board, and you will follow me.

But I reserve, for your sakes and mine own, the right to vote against a fight if I consider that the odds are too great against us. Let us not, through an exaggerated conceit, fall foul of one ship when we might sink six others through discretion. If, on the other hand, we find ourselves out-gunned and outmanœuvred, and fight we must—well, then, we will, and maybe get the victory.

Who knows?" Needless to say, Mipps had seen to it that Syn's property had all been returned. Shoes, coat, pistols and scabbard, and his sea-chest, still unopened, stood beside one of the bunks.

Mipps, who preferred a hammock to a bunk, insisted upon slinging it outside the cabin door.

"For," said he, "pirates or no, and co-commanders as you might say, I know my station. You was above me on the Marshes, and is so here. I'm twice the man I was when I met you. I always knew I was born for adventures, and you helped me to it with that loan. Without it the Customs would have caught me.

I've got it for you here, sir, and in English money." Mipps produced a key tied with a piece of tarty string round his neck and opened his sea-chest, upon which he had been sitting. From this he took a canvas bag, in which his fingers fumbled for a time, at last drawing out a small paper parcel, which he handed to his companion. Syn looked at it and laughed, for on it as scrawled, "Mipps his debt to Parson Syn."

"You'll find that all correct, sir," said Mipps. "And it brought me luck, that chance meeting with you."

"So you thought this piracy business luck, eh?" laughed Syn. "Well, perhaps you are right. If your life changed from that bright morning on Lympne Hill, why, so did mine. But my change was for the worse. That very morning started the blighting of my soul. That is why I journey to America, and I'll confess to you that as soon as we touch land I shall put this ship behind me and set out on my life's mission."

"What, give up piracy and go on a preaching mission? Oh, I say!"

"No, on a killing mission," corrected Syn. "I have journeyed to find an enemy. There is a man I have to kill. That is to be my great adventure. I am sorry I shall have to leave you to this life. As to this money, here it is. It was a gift, and I will not take it back."

"And I can be obstinate, too," grinned Mipps. "I never takes nothing for nothing."

"Then give me something in exchange," replied Syn; "brass buttons; a clasp knife—any trifle you can spare."

"Very well, sir," said Mipps seriously. "I'll give you something in exchange if you'll accept it. And the value I put it at is just three spades, two crowns, and a silver fourpenny. And this thing is myself. Just this Mister Mipps you see here in the cabin. Just a collection of bone, flesh, blood and gristle, and my clothes thrown in. We are bound for the slave country. A rough country, too, where a gentleman like yourself needs a servant. No need to tell you I'll be faithful. You know that. Well, what do you say, sir? Have you bought me? 'Cos if so I'll put this money back in my chest."

"You mean you'll give up piracy?" asked Syn.

"I mean that I am going to help you kill this man whoever he may be," replied the little man.

"I'll tell you who he is, and now," said Syn, and immediately recounted the whole business of his marriage and betrayal.

At the end of the tragic recital Mipps drew his sheath-knife and plunged it into the cabin table, crying out, "The dirty dog." He then flicked the handle of the quivering blade with his finger and added, "He won't be Happy Tappitt by the time we deals with him. Is the business of sale complete? Or do you think the price is too steep for my body and soul?"

"I think, my good Mipps, that I shall never make a better bargain in my life, and there's my hand on it." That night they laid their plans, agreeing to escape from the ship at the first opportunity.

"For the longer we remain amongst these rascals, the greater risk we run of hanging at the last," said Syn.

Outwardly, however, they stuck to their bargain with the pirates. In a few days Syn had established a stricter discipline than any pirate ship had ever boasted. The men respected him, because they feared him, and they sprang to his orders with a will. Besides this, he brought luck to the Sulphur Pit. Prize after prize fell to them: rich merchant ships whose wealth increased the pirates' shares beyond the dreams of the most covetous. In every attack Syn, as good as his word, led the boarding party to victory, and the pirates worshipped him for his bravery and skill, and the death of Black Satan was accounted the luckiest circumstance that could have happened to the ship. In Syn they not only had the most dashing commander, but one who also looked after his men carefully.

Their casualties were light, and many a man who might have

died from wounds had Black Satan been their captain owed his life to he careful nursing which Syn insisted on.

Much to their relief they never fell in with an English ship, for Syn and Mipps had made it clear that they would never countenance the plank for English sailors.

"That shred of decency we will at least reserve," as Syn had said to Mipps.

To all other crews, however, they were merciless. No one was left alive to tell the tale ashore.

But Syn had no intention of postponing his vengeance for too long in order to keep the seas, and at last he found the excuse to run for land. This was based on a report laid before the pirates by Mipps. The ship's bottom was growing too foul for any speedy manœuvring, he stated, and as soon as possible they ought to lie up some river for careening.

"I agree," said Syn. "Our guns are of no avail if we have no sailing speed. A spell ashore will be good for our souls, and when we have cleansed the jolly Sulphur Pit we shall sail out refreshed for new adventuring."

Aware that the careening operations were necessary, and looking forward to carouses ashore, the pirates were of a mind to set the course for land. It then remained to decide upon their place of call. Some were for the Tortugas, a place that had been much patronized by Black Satan. Others voted for the Bahamas, but Syn and Mipps, for their own private convenience, advocated the mainland of America. It would be more handy, they pointed out, not only for disposing of money safely, but also for the purchase of new supplies. At length it was decided to run for St. John's River, to the north of Florida, Dr. Syn volunteering to sail with Mipps in one of the ship's boats in order to find out if all was safe.

"I will take no risk of running the ship into a trap," he said. "While you anchor off the river mouth we will spy up the creeks, and see if there are any other vessels there that are unfriendly."

To this one of the pirates objected. "How do we know that you will return? It might be tempting to show your heels ashore, and we all agree that you are the leaders for us, and we don't intend to lose you."

"Do not let that trouble you," laughed Syn. "Neither Mipps nor I have shown ourselves dissatisfied, I think, and in order that all shall be fair and above board, we'll leave our share of the treasure in our cabin. After so much pains we should hardly abandon that." This satisfied them, and the course was set.

The winds being light, and the keel so very foul, it took them two weeks to reach the anchorage. Calling all hands Syn complimented them on their behaviour, and added that the time was now ripe for a royal drinking bout.

"We have been temperate, my lads, too long. We will now make up for lost time and dry throats. Drink as much rum as you can stomach, and Mipps and I will sail up river at dawn. We have shared out our portions of plunder fairly, and Mipps and I leave ours in your trust upon the cabin table. See to that, Mipps, and let who will inspect the bundles. No doubt we shall be back before you have outslept your drinking." The rascals needed no second bidding to attack the rum casks. In an hour they were well on the way to being very drunk. Syn went amongst them drinking and jesting, until he knew that there was no suspicion of their planned escape. The boat had already been lowered in readiness, and was alongside.

Mipps had stored their sea-chests, fresh water, provisions, ammunition and a compass. These precautions had not attracted much attention from the pirates, who were satisfied that both leaders had indeed left their share of plunder on the table.

"Maybe we'll have to lie low up river," explained Mipps. "In which case you wouldn't wish us starved."

There was no need to say farewell to their companions, for had they wished to it would not have been possible; for the whole crew were raving drunk by midnight, and before dawn were fast asleep. Even the watch were past all waking. Syn went the rounds pretending to be drunk himself, and was quite satisfied with what he saw.

"The sooner we start the better," he whispered to Mipps.

Syn stepped into the cabin to take a last look round, and to buckle on his sword. His eye fell on the table, and he saw that the bundles of their treasure had disappeared. When Mipps joined him for his cutlass he remarked on this.

"The rascals have moved them somewhere," he said.

"I put 'em in the boat," explained Mipps. "No use being too honest with dishonest men, and we'll need all we have to help us find this enemy of yours.

You get down in the boat, sir, and I'll follow. Got your pistols, sir?"

Syn nodded. "And I see you have. Oh, we shall do very well, I think." He left the cabin for the last time, went to the side and climbed the rope ladder down into the boat. "Hurry, man," he whispered, looking up the ship's side.

But Mipps had disappeared.

For some minutes he waited with what patience he could, and thinking something must be wrong, was about to climb aboard again when Mipps reappeared and scrambled down into the boat. "A little matter I had to see to, sir," he explained. "Ready, sir. Cast off." Syn took the tiller, and Mipps fell to the oars, pulling vigorously.

"Conserve your strength, man," advised Syn. "There's no need of such haste."

"Sooner we're away from them the better," replied Mipps.

"There's a breeze that will save you your pains," said Syn. "I'll up sail.

And, what is more, we'll change our plans. Since we are not watched by those drunken swine, we'll head up-coast. Why should we break our backs with trudging across difficult country with our sea-chests, when this boat can carry us right up to Charleston? The breeze will be behind us when we clear the promontory."

"Aye, aye, sir, that's game. I was wondering myself how the devil we was going to carry all this clodder without a horse and trap." The sail up and catching the wind, Mipps shipped his oars and the boat spanked along magnificently. When they were safely round the head of the river-bank, and headed north, Mipps sighed with relief.

"No danger now, sir," he said. "I was very anxious to get the head between us and the ship. You never know with all them drunken dogs about, and the magazine so full of powder."

"Tut, man, the magazine is locked and the key in our cabin," said Syn.

"They're not likely to want powder with so much rum in 'em."

"Well, I was only wishful of warning you, sir, that should the magazine blow up, don't get jumping and upsetting the trim. Queer things happens even on pirate ships. And the very name of Sulphur Pit puts one thinking of explosions." These words were hardly out of his mouth when the sky was reddened with flame, and a mighty roar rolled over the sea.

"Good God, man, that's the ship!" cried Syn.

"Must be," agreed Mipps. "It ain't the fifth of November, certainly. Good thing I warned you about trimming boat." Suddenly Syn suspected the truth. "Mipps," he said, "was that what you were doing when I was waiting in the boat? Did you go into the magazine?"

"Yes, sir, and I must have left a lighted candle there," he said shamefacedly.

"Very careless."

"And a train of powder, too, no doubt," added Syn grimly.

"Dead men tells no tales, sir," said the little man. "And you and I ain't going to hang for scum like that. I didn't want it on your conscience, sir, you being a parson and all, but when you think it over, you must own I took a good opportunity. We're clear now of the Sulphur Pit. Not a man could live through a bang like that, and I've done nothing but what a man-o'-war wouldn't have been proud to do. We've rid the seas of a very dirty mob. Confess, sir. Am I right? I'll be glad to know what you think."

"I think you're more of a little devil than I suspected. But if your case was put to the vote I believe the rights would be more than the wrongs."

"Thankee, sir," grinned Mipps. "You've took it handsome. And how about a nice little nip of rum to keep out the cold?"

"Aye, pass the bottle," answered Syn.

Chapter 13. Redskins

The two hundred miles from St. John's River to Charleston were navigated in less days than they had hoped to be possible. The breeze held steadily behind them and the weather fine, so that on the whole the voyage was pleasant. Clear of the pirates, they could now talk freely, and the liking which had always existed between the companions ripened into a real friendship. But no familiarity in Syn's conversation could break down the respectful attitude of Mipps, and the parson thanked God for his ally. By the time they sighted Charleston they understood each other well, and each knew that he could depend upon the other in any circumstances. They concocted a ringing-true story which Syn was to carry to the Governor, and during sailing hours he had rehearsed this over and over again, till both were satisfied. Each time some little detail was added, till on one occasion at the end of his recital Syn saw that the little pirate's eyes were filled with tears, and asked him what was wrong.

"It's so pathetic," blubbered Mipps. "I ain't had a cry for years. No, not since a friend of mine had an aunt what died what was very fond of him. And if our story you keep telling me was true, I think I should never stop crying. It's a most wonderful yarn, I considers, and if the Governor don't cry hisself silly over our misfortunes he's a cold pebble." But the Governor was no pebble. Indeed, he proved himself a very sympathetic friend. As luck would have it he was walking with a wealthy merchant on the quay when the wayfarers put in, and being curious as to what they were he sent a servant to inquire.

Now, although Mipps had considered it advisable to arrive in port dishevelled, dirty and unshaven, in order to heighten the effect of the imagined hardships they had undergone, Syn had insisted upon making a careful toilet before appearing.

"Elegance and cleanliness will gain more sympathy," he had argued. "In all tribulations a gentleman possessing fresh linen and a razor should take the pains to use them." It was obvious, therefore, to the Governor, as he watched Syn's striking figure coming towards him on the quay, that here was a man of parts, a gentleman. The manner in which he swept off his three-cornered hat and the dignity of his bow, confirmed the opinion, so that, without waiting for the stranger to speak, the Governor said heartily:

"Welcome to Charleston, sir, and the Carolinas. I am the Governor of the South State, and shall be honoured to know your name and business."

"My name is Christopher Syn, sir," he answered gravely, "and although my sword and pistols seem to give the lie to it, I am yet a Doctor of Divinity from our English Oxford." And thereupon he recited the story he had rehearsed so often to Mipps.

The Governor showed such commiseration over the fate of the ill-starred Intention, and also at the hardships which the pirates had inflicted upon the young parson and his faithful servant. But his pity was outweighed by joy on learning that Black Satan and his Sulphur Pit had gone to their last account, and he immediately invited Doctor Syn to accompany him to his house so that they could crack a bottle in celebration. Syn thanked him, but begged that he might first accompany his servant to some inn, in order that they might stow away such property as they had left them in the boat. The question of an inn the Governor swept aside, sending a servant to assist Mipps in disposing of the boat and conveying its contents to his own residence, in which he declared they should both stay till they had formed their further plans.

As far as Doctor Syn was concerned, things could not have fallen out better, since the Governor, being the best-informed man in the Colony, was the most likely to give him information concerning Nicholas. But he was sorry for Mipps, and told him so at the first opportunity.

"To think, my good Mipps, that you who have lorded it as a High Sea Adventurer should now be called upon to play the humble valet to an English parson." To which Mipps replied, "What does it matter, sir, what I does, as long as I does my duty? And my bounden duty is to serve you in all weathers and under all conditions. You bought me body and soul at my own pricing, and all I hopes is that you have not made the worse bargain."

During their stay at the Governor's Syn learned much about his enemy. At first the fellow had been liked well enough. He had spent money freely: perhaps too freely, for he was soon in money difficulties all over the town. His trading up-river was disappointing, and his name became connected with many scandals, both in trade and private life. The Governor did what he could, for, as he said, he was more than sorry for the beautiful young wife and son.

"For their sakes," he explained, "I managed to get the rascal out of the State with a whole skin."

"And have you any notion where they have gone?" asked Syn.

"His wife told me that her husband was attracted by the reports of good trading up the Hudson River, and there is certainly business to be done not only with the Indians, but also with the French. In which case the place to make inquiry would be Albany. I take it that you know the man, and perhaps wish to get in touch with him?"

"I was at Oxford with him," replied Syn. "Even there he had a way of getting into scrapes. But sometimes the cleverest rascal goes too far. Since the lady with him is my legal wife you will own that I have the strongest motive for getting in touch with him. And he will find that my touch will not be gentle."

"Perhaps I can help you," went on the Governor, "for my cousin, Colonel Clinton, is in command of the military in Albany. Between you I think this scoundrel could be brought to book." Three days later Doctor Syn took leave of the Governor, and armed with a letter of introduction to the Colonel, set sail with Mipps for New York, from whence they could proceed to Albany.

The captain of the vessel, who had been told by the Governor of the blowing up of the dreaded Sulphur Pit, never tired of questioning Doctor Syn and Mipps about Black Satan.

On reaching New York, the captain was commissioned to carry a cargo to Albany, so Syn and Mipps remained aboard and travelled with him up the broad Hudson.

On arrival Syn took lodgings at the best inn, and then deposited the bulk of their treasure in the vaults of an English Banking House. He then presented his letter of introduction to Colonel Clinton, from whom he learned that Nicholas had set out by canoe to trade with the Indian tribes. He had taken Imogene and the boy, as well as an Indian interpreter and guide. The Colonel advised Syn to await them in Albany, assuring him that, short of any disaster overtaking them, the party would return to the town on completion of business.

For weeks they waited patiently, during which time Doctor Syn, by preaching from the principal pulpits of the town, gained respect and popularity.

At last a letter came from the Governor of South Carolina which determined their stay at Albany, for the news it brought was disquieting. After the usual courtesies to himself and servant, and inquiries and kind messages to the Colonel, the letter went on to state that besides Syn and Mipps, who had so luckily escaped from the pirate ship in time, there had been one other survivor from the explosion.

I should be glad, my good Doctor, for any information you may have concerning him, for my task is difficult in knowing how to deal with him. From my description, I think you will not fail to remember him. He is a mulatto. As ugly as a looking devil as ever I clapped eyes upon. Thin to emaciation, with skin like cracked parchment. High cheek-bones and the most brilliant black eyes, which seem to shoot out the blackest hatred. His hair is deathly white. He understands no English, but we have been able to gather something of his story through the help of one of my slaves, a West Indies boy, who talks to him in the Cuban dialect. This has been the more difficult because our mulatto is dumb.

He lost the power of speech from the shock of the explosion. He arrived here in the most deplorable condition, half-starved and with bleeding feet, having walked along the coast. I have lodged him in the gaol, where my own surgeon is attending him, in the hope of recovering his speech. Then I could be the better judge of his integrity, for since you and your faithful servant have recounted so many details of the Sulphur Pit, I shall see if he is lying, should his story not agree with yours. In which case my judgment will be the harsher, whereas I now feel inclined to think that he has been punished enough for his piracy.

Both Syn and Mipps remembered the mulatto well, as a mutinous dog who had on many occasions threatened the discipline which they had imposed upon the pirates.

"But even if his tongue does wag again," said Mipps, "by the old man's letter he won't be believed, sir."

"We must take no chances of that," returned Syn. "For if this mulatto becomes too convincing, he may well upset our story, and we must not forget that he knows me as Syn the parson who turned pirate. I am therefore determined that Syn shall disappear. We will let people think that I have died. I shall tell my friends here that I have had a solemn call to preach the Gospel to the Redskins. When I do not return, they will no doubt give me a martyr's crown. Meantime we will go on searching for my enemy, who I believe does not intend returning to Albany. I rather think his instincts tell him that I am already on his track. In three days' time we shall be after him again. Are you willing to risk your scalp amongst the Indians?"

"It's your scalp. You bought it, sir," said Mipps. "In three days? Then I'd best be purchasing a canoe, a barrel of rum, and eatables."

"And I'll make inquiry for a reliable guide," said Syn.

Providing themselves with clothes more suitable for their journey, they packed their sea-chests with such properties as they wished to leave behind them, and deposited them in the same bank that was hoarding their treasure.

Syn then drew up an agreement with the banker that their property should be handed over to one or both of them on personal demand, but if neither of them came back within the year, the banker was to sell jewellery and all, to the best advantage, and to send the value to Solomon Syn, New Romney, England.

Having thus provided against emergency, Doctor Syn took leave of his many friends in Albany, and set a northern course up the Hudson.

The Indian, who went by the high-sounding name of "Mountain Cat", proved himself at once to be efficient, very strong, but also very silent.

Knowing that the pastor's object was to locate Nicholas and his party, he went to work in his own way, seeming unperturbed at what Syn and Mipps considered a gigantic and puzzling task. When Syn suggested they might hail such craft as passed them, and ask if the party they followed had been seen by them, he shook his head. He had his own method, and it was curious. He would frequently head for the bank, and that at places where his companions could see neither camp nor habitation, disappear into the forest, but to return after an interval and point once more with decision up-river. Syn let him go his own way, but Mipps became cynical.

"Funny way of going on, I calls it," he said when this method had gone on for some days and nights. "Where the devil does old Puss-cat get his information from? I never hears nothing but twitterings of birds and squawks of wild beasts."

"He's no doubt in touch with Indian tribes," said Syn. "They're a silent race, and shy at showing themselves."

"Unsociable, I calls it," replied Mipps.

On one occasion the method changed, for instead of pointing up-river he unpacked the canoe, hoisted it upon his shoulder, and signing them to carry the provisions set off through the woods. This was the prelude to an incessant toil.

Days and nights were spent in avoiding the worst swamps, threading a way through what seemed impenetrable undergrowth, on some occasions scaling precipitous rocks in order to reach some other river where the canoe could be refloated till its way was barred by thunderous waterfalls.

Through all these trials the Indian insisted not only that silence should be strictly observed, but also the greatest haste. At first they thought he did this in order to finish the contract the sooner, but they had yet to discover that his reason was the more alarming. They had been travelling fast for many miles down a turbulent river, when the Indian suddenly made for the shore. Above them hung a gaunt bare rock, which their guide climbed rapidly as soon as he had seen the canoe made fast. Syn and Mipps watched him, as his half-naked body squirmed its way to the top. He did not look over the crest of the crag, but lay still as though listening, but as Mipps whispered to his master, "What Pussy expects to hear with the noise of this damned trout-stream booming" was beyond their ken. Presently he came down cautiously, now and then stopping to remove the marks of his own feet. It was obvious to the others that this particular sport in the wilderness was known in every detail by "Mountain Cat", for no sooner had he rejoined them than he speedily unpacked the contents of the canoe and deposited them in a hole, which he covered with dried leaves. He then pointed to a large tree whose low branches interlaced with those of its neighbors. To the base of this tree he carried the empty canoe, which he leaned end up against the trunk. Then, grasping the mooring-rope he climbed to the first branches and then up to the second. The thickness of the leaves now hid him completely from night. The rope went tight, and the canoe, swinging clear of the truck, began to ascend after him. Syn and Mipps hastened to ease the weight of it till it was pulled too high for their reach.

"What does he want to go sailing in the tree-tops for?" whispered Mipps.

"No doubt he has sensed unfriendly Indians," replied Syn.

In a minute or so he had dropped once more to the ground, and indicating with a stick the surest notches on the surface of the trunk for hands and feet, indicated that they should climb it.

Up went Syn and Mipps, to find the canoe safely cradled across three stout branches, which formed the most admirable dry dock. Indeed, so secure was its position that the companions took their customary seats and waited. The Indian meantime busied himself by covering up the tracks which their trampling had caused from the river to the tree. He moved pebbles. He scattered leaves. He combed up crushed grass. Then he climbed the tree once more,

and as though it was the most ordinary thing to do, sat himself
solemnly in the canoe with the others, where he continued to sit
with a warning finger to his mouth, commanding silence.

Syn and Mipps could hear nothing but the tumbling waters of
the river, whose music they were forced to listen to for some half-
hour. It was characteristic of Syn that even in this extremely odd
and obviously dangerous situation he did not waste time. He
produced a volume from his pocket which had been given to him
by the compiler, a mission parson in Albany, who had done much
preaching to the Indians. This book contained a treatise upon the
manners of speech employed by the Red tribes, with a dictionary
of all the useful words and phrases. Since this worthy cleric had
collected his material from amongst the Adirondack Indians, it was
likely to be of greater service to Doctor Syn, who was now sitting up
a tree in that very territory, as he had learned from "Mountain
Cat."

Mipps spent his time in watching first his master and then the
Indian, who sat with eyes closed in meditation, but still holding his
finger to his lips. After a while the comicality of thus sitting in a
boat up a tree overcame the control of his sense of humour.
Attracting his master's attention he traced out invisible capital
letters upon the floor of the canoe, while tears of suppressed
laughter ran down his cheeks. Syn smiled too, for the little pirate
had written, after jerking his head towards the Indian, "Hush-a-by,
Baby, on the tree-top." Sensing a movement of the canoe which
Mipps caused at his writing and shaking through silent giggles, the
Indian, without opening his eyes, pointed first towards the rock,
and then straight down beneath them. Through tiny peepholes in
the thick foliage they looked. Upon the highest crag of the rock,
and silhouetted magnificently against the sky, stood a feathered
and warpainted Brave, shading his eyes against the sun, and
signalling with his murderous tomahawk to those beneath him.
These were in two files, one skirting the base of the rock and
trotting one behind the other, while the second file were passing
close by the very tree which concealed the canoe. This lot halted for
some minutes as though awaiting an order from the scouting
Brave, and the three men in the tree trembled lest one of them
should discover their property beneath the heap of leaves.
Fortunately they were too intent upon watching their leader, and
presently they moved out of sight as silently and as quickly as they
had appeared.

Their guide explained that these warriors were from beyond

the mountains, and were no doubt out after scalps from an enemy village in the next valley.

Till the battle was over it would not be safe to leave their retreat, he said, so he climbed down and collected food and drink from their covered hole.

Presently above the voice of the river they heard the war-cries and a mighty whooping and screaming, which continued persistently throughout the day. The Indian said it must have been a hard-fought fight, but could not judge which side had been the victors. At last the sun went down behind the mountains. The twilight was short, and dusk quickly gave place to a black night. "Mountain Cat" then decided to spy out the situation and to see whether or no it would be safe to continue on the trail. He would be back, he said, within the hour, and enjoined the Englishmen on no account to leave their hiding-place. So they waited with what patience they could, listening to the loud screamings of a wardance.

When the moon arose, Doctor Syn calculated that their guide had been absent some three hours, and feared that he had been either captured or cut off.

They then discussed whether or no they could go in search of him.

When they had waited a considerable time, and still no sign of the Indians, they climbed down from the tree, and set off.

Now, although the village was less than a mile away, they encountered the greatest difficulties in reaching it. In most places the undergrowth was breast high, and when overcome, led to one of the many impetuous mountain streams that had to be crossed upon slippery boulders, and it was actually dawn before they crawled over a hillock in the forest and looked down upon a clearing. It was evident that here had been the site of the village, but all that remained was charred wrecks of smouldering habitations. Beneath a number of blackened stakes erected in a rude circle lay many bodies that had been fired, while in the centre of this grim arena was a naked Indian tied to the trunk of a tree. He was still alive, for his limbs kept moving as he attempted to relieve the tight agony of the biting ropes that bound him. Around the clearing were ranked more than a hundred warriors, the very men who had passed the canoe the day before, because the Englishman recognized their leader who had stood upon the rock.

He was going from man to man, as though inspecting them. From every score or so he chose one, who stepped forward from the line. When the five had been selected, the Brave signalled to the rest, who turned and walked off silently into the woods. Syn and Mipps noted that the five were not so gaily decorated either with feathers or war-paint as their fellows who were marching. The Brave then advanced to the bound man, and with his knife severed the cords. The exhausted victim collapsed for a moment on the hard, beaten earth, but after rubbing his chafed limbs he stood up proudly and faced the Chief.

Having his back to the hillock where Syn and Mipps crouched, they could not see his face, but there was something in the bearing of his tall, gaunt frame which made them certain that this was indeed their missing guide.

"Those five rascals are to be his executioners," whispered Syn. "Compared to the others they are but youngsters and are no doubt about to prove their worth with blood-letting. Had the rest not gone, we should have been hard put to it to rescue our 'Mountain Cat', but this lot we can tackle. I think the Chief will follow his men and leave the dirty work to these cadets. If so we shall be rid of him the easier."

It was then that they saw the Chief advance to the victim and, with what seemed a gesture of courtesy, had him his own tomahawk. This looked a heavy weapon with a bright steel blade.

"He is allowing him the right to defend himself," whispered Syn, as he fingered the butts of his pistols. "And I was right in my guess. I believe he is about to follow the tribe." Indeed, the Chieftain had turned his back upon the prisoner and with majestic strides walked to the five young warriors, who at the same time began to execute fantastic steps, working themselves up into a frenzy for killing. The Chief halted some five paces in front of them, and raising both arms to the dawning sky appeared to be blessing their prowess. He was then some twenty paces from the armed prisoner, and still with his back to him.

It was then that they saw the man they took to be "Mountain Cat" take two steps forward, swinging the tomahawk, and with a mighty effort hurl it through the air. It struck the Chieftain with terrific force between the shoulder-blades, the steel of the axe actually severing the long tail of feathers from his headdress. The hands, uplifted as they had been in benediction, clawed the air convulsively, and then down he fell full length upon his face. Bereft of his weapon, the prisoner folded his arms and stoically awaited his death at the hands of the five. The sudden killing of their Chief, whom they took to be dead without examination, caused them to dance with the greater fury, and with each step they capered nearer to his slayer.

"Now, Mipps," said Syn. "You to his right side, I to his left. Pistols first, and then steel."

"No quarter, eh?" asked Mipps as they ran.

"None," replied Syn.

The whirling frenzy of the five did much to help the surprise attack of the Englishmen, who were on them before they could realize that their unarmed victim was now supported. Then they rushed altogether. Syn brought down his two flank men by firing his pistols simultaneously and practically at point-black range. Mipps fired his right pistol, and hit, but did not kill, so, quickly changing over by dropping the discharged weapon and grabbing the other with his right hand from his left, he used the second charge upon the same attacker killing him then outright, and hurling his pistol in the face of the next attacker, which checked him for a second and enabled Mipps to draw his cutlass, a weapon with which he had made himself acquainted aboard the pirate ship.With it he met the murderous blow of the tomahawk, and ran his second man through the stomach with the point. The middle man rushed not at Syn but at the Indian, and had not Syn's long blade darted in between his ribs the Chieftain's death must have been avenged. As it was, the rescued Indian by refusing to leap back in the face of his enemies, received a bad flesh cut in the leg as his attacker fell dead. From body to body went Syn passing his sword through the heart of each, and crying out to Mipps that they must get to cover quickly, lest the noise from their pistols should bring the tribe back.

Mipps made a strange reply: "Well, I'll be damned!" he said.

"And why?" demanded Syn, as he cleaned his blade with a handful of dust.

Mipps scratched his head and pointed to the Indian. "Why, sir, this 'ere ain't Mister Pussy at all." Syn looked and said, "By gad you're right! It's not 'Mountain Cat'."

"'Mountain Cat' scalped and burned," said the Indian in English. "Me knew him. Good guide same as me. Speak English both. Me Shuhshuhgah. Mean Blue Heron. Son of Chief two mile there." He pointed in the direction taken by the warriors. "Them bad men may return. We hide a time. This way. Quick." He took a step forward, but fell because of the wound in his right leg. Syn saw that the muscle of the calf had been severed, so telling him to put his arms around their shoulders, they dragged him to the cover of the woods. At the foot of the hillock over which they had crawled to the attack, Shuhshuhgah pointed to a curtain of thick overhanging creeper, behind which was a cunningly hidden cave. Into this they crept, while Syn, tearing a strip from his shirt arm, bound up the Indian's leg.

As it happened, they had only just got to cover in time, for the noise of the pistols had caused a party of the warrior tribe to return to see what was amiss.

When the fugitives peeped through the creeper they saw them, three men standing over the body of their Chieftain. They removed the tomahawk and turned him over on to his back. Then they examined the bodies of the five dead cadets, and seemed bewildered at not finding the body of Shuhshuhgah. Then, taking the tomahawk with them and picking up the feathered tail that had been cut from their Chieftain, they trotted off with wild cries into the wood, following the direction of their fellows.

After waiting for some little time for the scouts to get clear, during which time Syn and Mipps re-charged and re-primed their pistols, Shuhshuhgah proposed that they should set out for his father's village, which no doubt the war-trail party was now attacking.

"But you should not walk, even with our help," said Syn. "Besides, we shall find ourselves at a disadvantage coming up behind them with our way to your village cut off."

"Under them we shall walk," explained the Indian. "There is a secret way into my father's camp." They selected two wigwam poles that had escaped the burning, and with the long sheath-knife belonging to Mipps had soon cut and bound some strong tendrils of the climbing creeper that abounded in the woods. Placing the Indian upon it, this was easy to carry stretcher-wise.

They followed the Indian trail through the woods, which made it easier and quicker travelling. When they had gone about a mile they once more heard the war-cries of the warriors. These cries growing louder and louder as they advanced, Shuhshuhgah at last pointed to a thick clump of bushes that fringed the trail.

"Put me down," he whispered. "We crawl through them. Then pick up secret trail." They set down the stretcher, and upon his stomach the Indian began to crawl through, followed by Syn and Mipps, dragging the stretcher after them. After some twenty-five yards of this difficult passage they came out upon another trail, when the Indian was once more put upon the stretcher and carried on.

Presently they heard the lowing of cattle mingled with the war-cries, and at the same time the trail, which had been rising steadily, reached a summit heavily overshadowed by trees. Up this the Indian crawled from the stretcher, and, after peering over cautiously, motioned the others to leave the litter below and join him. From this vantage they looked down upon a grassy plateau where some two hundred head of cattle were grazing, guarded by three or four mounted Indians, who trotted their shaggy ponies backwards and forwards along the slope to prevent the cattle roaming into the range of arrow fire from the stockaded village. From the height where they crouched, the three fugitives could see the main body of the attacking force awaiting the order to advance against the pallisades in the shelter of a dried-up river-bed. Shuhshuhgah whispered that his father would await attack, and then spare some half of his braves to run through the tunnelled secret path which came out into a cave at the base of the very hillock upon which they now waited. The enemy were dancing safely in the river-bed, working themselves up into the required frenzy for attack.

It was then that Mipps made what seemed to Syn an entirely irrelevant remark, but which was destined not only to spell disaster to the attackers, but to coin a name which was to become fearful enough to terrorize the trade routes of the high seas.

Mipps pointed to Shuhshuhgah's blood-stained bandage and whispered, "'Ere, look at that big beast. Enjoying a good meal off your blood, Shushy mate." The Indian looked at his leg, and saw what to the others was a large gad- or horse-fly. He took the fearful insect very carefully between his finger and thumb, and with a smile of triumph said, "It is the Clegg. Terrible fellow too.

You shall see what he can do. Look." He flung it into the air over the lip of the hillock in the direction of the cattle. They saw it flying and heard its waspish note. The cattle sensed its coming. Panic seized them. This fly was their worst enemy, for it was too small to trample or toss, and yet large enough to suck their blood and cause the most maddening irritation. A mediaeval knight in full armour might have felt the same toward a flea. Bellowing in panic, they stampeded for the riverbed in full gallop, sliding down the bank in terror right amongst the dancing Indians, who feel and scattered before the giant impact. The by now invisible Clegg fly kept the cattle on the run, and, like a sheep-dog, kept them well herded, so that as they were driven down the river-bed they presented a solid wedge of hoof and horn. The defending Indians, seeing what had happened, gave the attackers no time to rally, but attacked in their turn, swarming over the pallisades and hurling themselves upon their trampled enemy, who had no chief to encourage them. It was then that Shuhshuhgah pointed beneath them, and round the base of the hill there came trotting a long line of fresh warriors.

"They came by the tunnel," he said. "I thought my father would use it."

Taken now on both sides of the river, the deep bed became a human shambles. The carnage was ghastly.

"Your Mountain Cat is avenged," said the Indian.

"Poor old Pussy!" replied Mipps.

In a few minutes the victory was complete, and Shuhshuhgah's village was safe. It was then that he raised himself upon his elbow and gave the cry of the heron three times. Those who saw him waving ran to the hillock.

To these Shuhshuhgah explained how his life had been saved by the two pale-faces, telling them to bring him the litter and carry him by way of the tunnel to his father.

This tunnel, as Syn and Mipps discovered, was entered through a cave on the side of the hill, and with torch-bearers to light the way they descended a flight of rock steps into a long, wide passage. The Englishmen walked each side of the litter, for the Indian had given a hand to each in order to show good faith.

Presently they reached another flight of steps and, climbing this, reached a rough doorway, which by the light of the torches they saw was hung with a curtain of skins. Parting this, the torch-bearers called out:

"Shuhshuhgah lives." They found themselves in a vast cavern, into which their wounded were brought and attended to by the women. Amongst these there walked an elderly man of great height and fine presence. It did not need the Indian to tell them that this was his father, and the Chieftain. The venerable warrior turned to the torchbearers, and watched the stretcher carried in. Then, approaching, he said:

"Shuhshuhgah." Syn and Mipps were standing aside to allow the father to embrace his son, whom he must have thought dead, but the son would not allow this. Instead he placed the Englishmen's hands upon those of the Chief, and in the Indian tongue told how they had risked their lives and saved his. The old man replied with fitting thanks, which Syn not only understood, but answered, much to their astonishment, in the same language.

Mipps said, "'Ere, sir, I'm missing all this. Wish you'd talk English." After Shuhshuhgah's leg had been re-dressed, the Chieftain conducted them to his own hut, and gave them rum and light flour-cakes. Mipps, who was a good trencherman at any time, swallowed his portion in two mouthfuls and looked around for more.

At this Shuhshuhgah smiled and said, "Do not spoil your stomach for the victory feast, my little brave. There will be eating and dancing to the fill by sunset. Do you not smell the cattle roasting?" Mipps sniffed and nodded, and stayed his gnawing stomach with that reflection. He was glad, however, to find that there was no such restriction put upon the rum, in that it was as powerful as fire.

All this while the warriors were returning with scalps. The cattle had been rounded up, and the oxen upon the spit poles were roasted. With great ceremony the Chief sat, with his son, Syn and Mipps around him. Before the feast started, the singing poet of the tribe sang of the killing, thanking God for the bravery of the pale-faces who had saved their beloved Shuhshuhgah, whose own ingenuity with the Clegg fly came in for many stanzas of praise. There followed a dance, in which the scene was re-enacted, and with great effect, since Syn and Mipps, falling into their humour, loaned not only their jackets and three-cornered hats to those representing them, but sword and cutlass as well. Mipps having no stature, a little boy was picked to dance his part, and Mipps applauded this urchin's caperings more than any. This and the rum so excited his admiration that upon the conclusion of the dance Mipps leapt to his feet and, shouting a nautical tune, executed a very spirited hornpipe, to the wonder of the Indians.

The feast itself went on for hours, during which, with much strange ceremony, Syn and Mipps were made blood-brothers of the tribe, and given many a pipe of peace. Indian trophies of value were presented to them, Mipps being specially delighted with a barrel of rum for his own consumption.

"This is the life for me, sir," he told his master. "Better than being pirate.

When I hornpiped aboard the Sulphur Pit—the devil rot its timbers—an extra allowance was all we could expect. But a barrel. This must be that there place in the Psalms we used to sing about in Dymchurch choir, 'Land flowin' with milk and honey', but better, since I always had more taste for rum than milk." A spacious hut had been placed at their disposal, and just before dawn Syn and

Mipps retired to it for a much-needed rest. For some time Syn lay on his back upon a comfortable couch of grass and skins and with his eyes to the thatched roof he thought. At last, seeing that Mipps had opened one eye from his bed at the other end of the hut in order to pat his barrel of rum, and to take from it a further night-cap, Syn said:

"I have found my new name, Mipps. When Syn disappears into the death which I have invented for him I shall live on as one Clegg. I shall drive that Nicholas into a panic, just as that fly drove the cattle before him. I think now we shall have no difficulty in finding the rascal. These tribesmen of ours will scent him out for me. How do you fancy serving Captain Clegg?"

"It's a good enough name, sir," replied Mipps, "so long as Doctor Syn ain't really turned his parson's toes up. I'll serve him. But don't go altering my name. I'd forget all about it in my next drunk."

"Very well, then Captain Clegg and Mister Mipps let it be," said Syn.

"Harking back, Mipps, to that morning upon Lympne Hill when we first met, I don't think we imagined that we should be sleeping like this by the light of Red Indians' fires."

"If they worries you, sir," said Mipps, "I'll blow 'em out."

"No, let them bide. I like red fire," chuckled Syn. "I carry so much in my heart. Red hate, Mister Mipps. Red hate."

"Aye, sir," replied Mipps. "But when we spits this Nicholas through his gizzard, what then? Are you for home and pulpits again, or for more of these jovial adventures?"

"I will tell you that answer when our enemy is dead. Till then we follow.

Our way may be short or long."

Chapter 14. Clegg's Harpoon

The next words of Doctor Syn's Odyssey can be best described in his own words, which he penned at sea to his friend Antony Cobtree of Dymchurch. As things befell, however, it took many a long year reaching its destination, for having taken the pains to write it, the Doctor's caution persuaded him to keep it back, and it lay in his sea-chest till he ultimately returned to Romney Marsh.

My dear Tony (it read), In the hopes of meeting with some home-bound ship, which may carry these lines to you, I am writing in my cabin aboard the whale-ship Ezekiel, which is at the moment lying becalmed in the Southern Pacific.

More moons ago than I care to count, I wrote to you of our adventures with the Redskins. Should it reach you, you will by this have read how my bloodbrothers of the tribe got news of our enemy and of how Shuhshuhgah, whom no arguments of mine could induce to stay behind, your humble servant, and my faithful Dymchurch carpenter, Mipps, set out upon his trail.

We got on our enemy's track easily enough, and followed him, sometimes hard upon his heels. Even in the larger towns we found that Nicholas had not kept quiet, and we could always depend upon some gossip concerning him at the chief inns. It was in one of these that a garrulous landlord told us that our friend the Captain journeyed with his wife and son towards the little port of New Bedford in Massachusetts, where he intended to fit out a trading vessel, which he would sail himself. This gossip rang true to me, when our Indian told me that from this port there sailed many a whale-ship for long voyages. Since these ships have no destination but whales, Nicholas would think such a voyage a good means of giving me the slip. Other gossipers confirming this, we set our horses' heads for this same port. On reaching it, we made our way to the harbour, where we saw one of these whale-ships casting off. We watched her as she cleared the roads for the open sea. A sturdy little craft, but pretty too under her full-set canvas. Mingling with the crowd, who were whale-minded to a man, we learned that her name was Isaiah. We watched this valiant little vessel disappear upon her hunting quest, and then proceeded to an inn, where we made inquiries concerning Nicholas. As you know, I am, my dear Tony, something of a fatalist. Well, I needed all my philosophy then; for would you credit it? The Isaiah had been purchased by Nicholas, and he had manned her with experienced whalemen, and we had seen her sail not knowing that he was aboard. And, Tony, he had taken her with him and the boy. At first I could have wept for rage, but my philosophy told me that I, too, must buy a share in some other ship and follow. My companions agreed that there was nothing else to do. I knew, of course, that I could count on Mipps to accompany me, but when I thought to take a fond farewell of our Indian I was mistaken. He had married a girl from amongst the Gay-head Indians who inhabit the beautiful island named 'Martha's Vineyard', a tribe who from time immemorial have fought the great leviathan. He proposed that we should journey there, and then cross to the next island of Nantucket, from which port he had been told the fastest and the largest whale-ships sailed. A thriving town, too, with much reliable wealth.

Indeed, so prosperous was this whaling trade that we could find no owner willing to sell us a vessel outright.

At last, however, I struck a bargain with a famous family of the trade named Coffin, by insuring the safe return of a vessel called Ezekiel, which was to be handed back with half profits upon the conclusion of the voyage. In this way the Coffins stood to gain, but not to lose. However, their experience was invaluable, for they found us a full complement of tried men with a captain of their own whose integrity they vouched for. I sailed on the ship's papers as half owner for the voyage, who wished to study the art of the harpoon. Mipps was shipped as carpenter, and Shuhshuhgah, who had never been to sea, as a Greenhorn. On this good ship we have now been to sea for two whole years. We have rounded the dreadful Horn in storms as mighty as the ever-growing hate in my heart. We have beat about Good Hope and killed fine whales there, and now we are back again after sperm whale in the Pacific, which has so far proved to be our most successful hunting-ground. But I hunt other than a whale. As I sharpen my blade I think only of plunging it into his black heart.

Two days later, Tony; for we have been hard driven cutting up two mighty animals. Both of them forty-barrelled Jonahs, and in one a pleasant lump of ambergris. I will not weary you with whaler's jargon, though some day I will write you a treatise on the subject. I love a good harpoon! It is a godlike weapon. Mine is a marvel, and I trust no whale will rob me of it, for I hope one day to send it crashing into human ribs. Aye, into Nicholas.

Exhausted, we looked around upon an empty sea, for we had been towed far out of sight from the lofty masthead of the ship, and there was nothing for it but to lie alongside our valuable corpse till morning. A salt breeze now fanned us, so that we were the more hopeful that the Ezekiel's sails would fill enough to follow us. We were far too weary to commence the tedious business of towing back our prize. Also it was easier for the ship to find us than for us to locate the ship. So we rigged what is known as a wall-pole. This is a slender mast which is thrust into the dead whale's spout hole, and a lighted lantern hoisted to its head. As the night set in under a clear moon, Shuhshuhgah pointed towards the horizon, and we saw white canvas moving up into the sky-line. At first we took this to be the mother ship searching for its lost child, but as her rigging mounted higher, our old oarsman contradicted us.

'That ship, don't listen for the clacking of an old woman's needles in Nantucket,' he said. 'A New Englander she may be, but not from our port. No.

You can tell by the set of her.'

We all devoutly hoped he was right, for the vessel never showed her hull above the horizon, and our little flicker from the lantern was evidently lost to her look-out in the dancing moon-sparks on the sea. Scratching for the breeze, she changed here course and tacked down below the line again, and we were once more alone.

All that night we lay beside our dead antagonist. Before dawn the breeze had freshened, and as the sun came up so did the sails of the Ezekiel, and we were safe.

Our carcase lashed safely alongside the Ezekiel, I left the cutters at work to take a glass of grog with the captain. He had a story to tell. Having seen my whale-boat charioted so ferociously out of sight, the captain had taken our direction before attending to the other boats, one of which lost their whale through the depth of its soundings, so that they had to cut the line for their life, and the other killing quickly the fine fellow to ours. He was waiting for the breeze to bring him nearer to us, when he sighted the very ship which we had seen. A whaler, too, but with every tun overflowing, and so bound for home rejoicing.

Aye, my good Tony, let me if possible anticipate your guess. She was the Isaiah from New Bedford. Our Nantucketer had been correct. Had he but known her name, I would have abandoned our carcase and rowed for her, to get my reckoning. But let me tell you in the captain's words. 'She signalled us for a Gam.' (This, my good

Tony, is a word for a high seas courtesy call between two captains.) 'They lowered a boat, and, much to my amazement, when the boat was manned and the captain standing at the helm an admiral's cradle was lowered bearing a woman. It was his captain's wife. She was very beautiful, and still but a girl, though when she was hauled aboard us she told me that her little son was asleep in her cabin. The captain was a pleasant enough fellow in his cups, and they were plentiful. He owned his ship and had done well for himself and the crew. You may believe that I anxiously questioned him about your whale-boat, and whether he had seen it. He had not. After that all went merrily over drinks, but being anxious about your fate, I kept referring to you as one of the most outstanding harpooners I had shipped with. It was when I described you that his wife seized his arm and whispered. At once a cold fear seemed to possess both. The reason I cannot explain. Immediately they insisted upon departure. I tried to dissuade them, for in the morning I had hoped they would have aided our search for you. However, go they would. On parting I learned his name was Nicholas Tappitt.' Tony, had I not chased that whale, I could have harpooned him in the cabin of the Ezekiel—in front of her eyes, too. But I learned further things from our captain, without in any way rousing his suspicions. Things that may prove useful to me. Nicholas upon the voyage has subjected his body to the stupid torture of the tattooist. He is a mass of symbols and designs: tattooed from head to foot. It will make him at least the more noticeable, and many inquiries after him the easier. He is now for home, or rather, his home port. But, as he said over his cups, he is no more for the whaling. He thinks to sail his ship into the Caribbean Seas. He sees great promise in piracy, I gather. Our captain considered this but drunken boasting. I have my own opinion. Well, if his black conscience takes him there through fear of me, it is there that I shall follow.

Who knows, Tony, but that your college friend, so blinded with hate, which is all-consuming, may not also hoist the Jolly Roger, and, like a lone shark, prey on pirate ships till I can kill him?p

Chapter 15. Syn Hoists the Black Flag

Four years after the Ezekiel had sailed from Nantucket, she returned fullladen with the richness of many a great whale. The Coffins were more than pleased with the results, and treated Captain Clegg generously. The Nantucket Bank, which they owned, had invested his money credited from Albany well, so that when Syn and Mipps sailed from the island for the port of New Bedford they were richer men. Here they learned that Nicholas had sold the Isaiah for a good sum, and had departed for the Western Indies, where he proposed to buy another vessel and with letters of marque go privateering.

"I doubt whether he will trouble about the letters," said Syn to Mipps. "Like as not his privateering will be black piracy. Well, we know something of that game ourselves." After so long at sea, Shuhshuhgah felt a hunger for his forests, but could only be persuaded to visit his people when Syn selected a rendezvous for a future meeting. Mipps, having been a professional pirate, was able to supply the very place. There was a thriving tavern in Santiago which was a popular sorting house for all the pirate news. The landlord of "The Staunch Brotherhood" was a discreet man, who could keep a secret so long as he was paid to do so. To this place Shuhshuhgah was to repair whenever he felt ready to rejoin Syn. Should Syn be at sea, the Indian, who was well provided with money, was to remain at this tavern till summoned.

On their journey through the Islands, Syn discovered that Nicholas had also gone to Santiago.

"Which shows," said Mipps, "that he's turned pirate. It's the chief occupation of that there town." On their arrival, Syn found "The Staunch Brotherhood" to be a large, rambling inn, built in the Spanish style with a large courtyard opening out upon the harbour front. It was openly the resort of pirates from all nations, where the roughest sailors jostled against rich owners and gaudily dressed captains.

Riotous quarrels and the heaviest drinking were the order of its days and nights. From his first entrance into this place, Captain Clegg, with Mipps at his heels, made himself felt, for he swaggered through the noisy crowd and in a ringing voice demanded the immediate service of the landlord.

"I am Pedro the landlord," answered a great, fat, greasy-looking rascal, who was wise enough to size up a man before dealing with him. "In what way can I serve you, Se—or?"

"I propose staying in this town upon important business," replied Syn, speaking rapidly in Spanish. "I have heard this inn of yours spoken of by my friend here as the best place for keeping one's sword-hand in practice. Also that your drinks are of the best. I hope for your sake that they are. My immediate demand is that you show me the best set of your apartments, after which I shall sample your wines."

"I will certainly show you my best rooms," returned Pedro. "They are very fine. Indeed, so fine that I have to make a small charge of one gold piece to show them."

"Travellers must pay, and landlords must live," said Syn pleasantly. "Here are two gold pieces. I am a generous man, but like my own way in things, though I am willing to pay for it in reason. Lead the way." Taking care to hide his face from the newcomers, Pedro bestowed a sly wink towards his friends nearest, and led the way to the outside staircase. Unlocking a door that opened upon a wide balcony, he led the strangers into a set of three well-furnished rooms.

"These are my best rooms," he said. "Since you have paid for the privilege you are welcome to look at them."

"I have looked at them, and think they are magnificent," replied Syn casually. "I desire no better. I take them. Now bring us wine, and I will see that our trappings are brought from the ship."

"That is not possible," said the landlord suavely. "These rooms are taken by a rich customer of mine. You paid to see. You have seen."

"Faith, sir, if this is a jest," retorted Syn sharply, "you will find the laugh against you. Why should I waste my time viewing rooms if not to take them.

Indeed I have taken them."

"But you see those two chests, Se—or," went on the landlord, "they belong to the occupier, who has gone with his wife and son to view the ship he has had built for him. Look, here are his wife's garments hanging in this cupboard. The press there is also full of their finery. He is an ugly man to cross, this great captain." Mipps looked at Syn, and saw a grim smile on his lips as he said, "An ugly man to cross, eh? Well, so am I, and should this rascal captain with his wife and boy be tattooed from head to foot, he'll find me yet the uglier."

"He has many, very many tattoo marks," said Pedro; "but if you take a word of caution, Se—or, from one who knows him well—" Syn interrupted with, "Take out his things, sir. I take these rooms."

"But, Se—or—" he began again.

"There are no 'buts' about it, my good man," interrupted Syn again. "Mipps, put the chests in the passage there and heap the clothes upon them. They must find room elsewhere. As for you, Master Pedro, there will be no trouble unless I make it for you. I am accustomed to be obeyed. Is this man called Nicholas Tappitt, Nikolino Tappittero or what? He has a habit of changing his name, I hear."

"The captain is known here as 'Black Nick'," returned the landlord.

Syn laughed. "Then tell Black Nick when he returns that others have the habit of taking what does not belong to them as well as he. You'll find he'll understand. If he starts trouble send him up."

"May I tell him your name, Se—or?" asked the landlord.

"Captain Clegg," replied Syn. "We will now drink wine together, so make haste and bring the best. Red wine for blood, and see that it is good. Bring rum, too, to wash it down with. But first help my man there with that chest. It looks heavy." Pedro looked at Mipps as he took one end of the great chest and said, "You have been here before—yes?"

"Been to most places, I have," returned Mipps in bad Spanish.

When everything had been cleared and placed in the passage, the landlord brought the drinks.

"Mind, Se—or," he said, "I take no responsibility for what Black Nick will do to you."

"But I take full responsibility for what I shall do to him," replied Syn. "And now give me your key of this main door. I have no mind to have any enter when we are out. We are going now to get our baggage. Here is gold in earnest of our good faith with you. That should carry our credit for some days," and he threw down on the table a handful of gold pieces.

Then, locking the door, and closely followed by Mipps, Syn swaggered out upon the quay.

Even amongst that crown of gorgeously dressed adventurers who thronged the harbour, Syn stood out by reason of his magnificent elegance and striking appearance. He wore a scarlet velvet suit trimmed with silver braid, and round the waist of the full-skirted coat a silver sash that held his pistols. His high three-cornered hat boasted a fine ostrich feather, while his long legs were encased in perfectly fitting thigh-boots, and as he strode along, the slender fingers of his left hand rested easily upon the large, chased, silver hilt of this long sword.

When Mipps went to engage porters to carry their chests from the ship which had brought them there, and which was now busily unloading, Syn approached a group of richly dressed adventurers who were seated at a pavement table beneath the awning of a wine-shop. Swinging his hat off and bowing royally, he asked them in Spanish to do him the honour of drinking with him. Nothing loth, for they were already curious to know who he might be, they accepted with politeness, and Syn called for the best wine and sat down.

He told them he was Captain Clegg, and had arrived in Santiago but an hour. He was here on shipping business, he said, and did any of them know a Captain Nicholas Tappitt, who went by the name of "Black Nick"? They smiled, and one of them answered that "Black Nick" had been the last name in their mouths.

"Perhaps, Captain Clegg, I can explain the better," replied the youngest of the party, a good-looking Spaniard, who, though dressed very foppishly, had a manly bearing which Syn admired. "I am under a commission for this Captain Nicholas," he went on. "I know the man personally, whereas these friends of mine only know of him by reputation, which I agree is not of the best. They have been advising me to have nothing to do with him, but I am one capable of looking after myself and for the best advantage. I will take a chance hand with fate always, Se—or, and so long as this or that employer serves my turn, I serve him. You see that vessel anchored there beyond the harbour mouth? He had her built. Yesterday she did her trial sailing trip. She is superb. I am in love with that ship, though not so partial to her captain, this Black Nick. But he has something of a genius for ships, though, as I tell him to his face, not so good a genius for dealing with men. I find myself in position of first mate. I have a full crew aboard, and not one of them who is not discontented or ever we put for sea. Black Nick wants all for nothing. He has got the crew aboard under false pretence. Their share of profit accruing from adventures is reduced to the minimum. They risk their necks at the yard-arm of any Government ship for a mere pittance. I see trouble. But the ship is sweet. Her guns are good. Her speed amazing. She has it in her to escape or to attack, according to the captain's mood. She is all ready for sea, and has been so these last four days.

We only wait for Black Nick himself. He is transacting business with a gentleman from Havana, a rich planter and ship-owner, who is staying with the Governor of this Town. We are to be sailing consort with two ships of his from Havana." Syn nodded. "And your crew are no doubt the more discontented at being kept aboard when they might be drinking ashore?"

"Aye, and another thing," went on the Spaniard. "The Black Nick is to bring his wife aboard. And the men say, 'Petticoats for all or none.'"

"To be sure petticoats are damned bad things on ships," said Syn. "And where will I find this Black Nick before he sails?"

"The Governor's house is some two miles out in the country. He took his wife and son out there this morning, I believe. They are to sleep there the night, which means a further delay and more flame to feed my men's anger. I am now bound for The Staunch Brotherhood Inn, where he promised to leave the orders.

I delayed here purposely in order to miss him if possible."

"I see that you have no love for him," said Syn. "I also see that my faithful servant has collected my baggage ad engaged porters there. Since we lodge at 'The Staunch Brotherhood', perhaps you will accompany us there." So, taking leave of the others, they sauntered along the quay, followed by Mipps and the porters.

Arrived at the inn, Pedro led Syn aside. "You had scarce been gone a moment when they returned. They had seen you passing on to the quay. As I was hastening to lighten the news about their rooms, they cut me short with orders as though they were in a great panic. No blame at all they gave me. They asked me how long you would be gone, and when I told them you were but collecting your baggage from your ship, they opened this chest and packed the pile of clothes into it in the greatest hurry. All this while they kept the Governor's carriage waiting for them. When they had locked the trunks, Black Nick gave orders that Juan Tarragona (whom your honour is now with) was to see their baggage upon his ship, the St. Nicholas, and wait for them to board sometime upon the morrow. They asked me to say nothing about these rooms which you had compelled me to give you. Your honour will therefore respect my very good faith and not betray me. Your honour has treated me well."

"I shall say nothing, friend Pedro," returned Syn, smiling at the man's roguery. "And you in your turn will say nothing of this to Se—or Tarragona. I will give him his captain's orders myself. And now, a word of advice to you.

You will do yourself no harm in keeping faith with me in the future, for I shall be the means of putting much gold into your treasure-chests. Now repeat the orders he left for that officer."

"That he would carry the baggage aboard the St. Nicholas; keep the ship ready for sea, as his business was sure to be completed by tomorrow or the next day at the latest. Then the St. Nicholas is to sail towards Havana, enter the Gulf of Batabano, to the south of it, where the treasure-ships for escort would be waiting behind the Island de Pinos. That is exact."

"I will tell him," said Syn. "And you remember to keep silent, unless he asks for confirmation. I shall be leaving you today, but if during my absence an American Indian called 'The Blue Heron' should ask for me, you will say that Captain Clegg is aboard his ship the Imogene. He will hear of her, I promise you, and so will you. The Indian can join me aboard when he learns where she lies, and in the meanwhile await news here at my expense." After making Pedro repeat these instructions, Syn sent him to order two riding-horses to take him and his servant to the Governor's house outside the town. He then rejoined Tarragona with the news of Black Nick's orders, which he altered to serve his own purpose.

"Black Nick left messages for both of us with the landlord. You are to take his baggage aboard the St. Nicholas immediately. You will also so me the kindness to take mine too, for I am to sail with you to Havana. Now between ourselves, my friend, I am a very wealthy man, and if I like the ship's behaviour upon this trip I shall make Black Nick an offer for her. He wishes us to go aboard and keep ready for sea, as he will join us in two days' time."

"Ah, no," cried Tarragona. "A further delay will mean a mutiny. It was with difficulty that I persuaded the men to keep ship today. If we do not sail tonight, they will overpower the officers and take to the boats. Then we shall have a fine drunken crew ashore, I promise you."

"Leave it to me," said Syn. "You go back with the baggage—mine and Black Nick's. I am going to ride out now to talk to him at the Governor's house.

I and my servant will be back within two hours, and I warrant I'll bring Black Nick along with us. After what you told me about his wife, I shall persuade him to leave her behind. One woman upon a long voyage is dangerous to a crew of rough morals. Now, what like are these two ships that we are to consort?"

"There again," cried out Tarragona. "Somehow the news is out amongst my crew that we are to take these treasure-ships to Spain. They even know their names, the Santa Mariana and the Santa Celesta. To speak frankly, the men aboard the St. Nicholas are pirates of the worst type, and this voyage with but little profit to them seems of too peaceful an order. They are grumbling that he got them aboard with fine promises, and then, when signing came, their pay was cut down to the minimum." Syn nodded. "Go back to your ship and tell them that they have a good adventurous friend in me. I will force Black Nick to reconsider his terms with the crew. Every man aboard shall have a more generous wage, and in addition a share of the profits. You may tell them if there is one man that Black Nick fears it is Captain Clegg, who sails with them and knows how to respect good sailors.

Up to this moment he has had more from me than I from him, but now I will turn the tables. You and I will stand together on this voyage, and the men will stand behind us. Go and tell them so. Should Black Nick not agree to my terms —and I have that over him to force his hand—I will compel him to sell the ship to me. I can buy it at his price. On the other hand, I think he will sell it at mine.

Within two hours, we will be aboard and shaking out the canvas." After seeing Syn and Mipps ride off towards the Governor's, the young Spanish officer, delighted at not having to return to the ship with tales of more delay, but rather with a fine sop to throw to his discontented men, escorted the baggage to his waiting boat, and was pulled off to the ship.

Meanwhile Syn and Mipps rode out of the town with a show of great haste.

At last, safely hidden beneath the trees of a grassy bridle-path, Syn drew rein.

"That ride has done us good," he laughed. "But I think we will not approach the Governor's House any nearer, though it needs all my patience not to ride there in hot haste and finish with Black Nick. I am not in the mind, however, to put him out of his misery so soon. We can torture him better by waiting. He has had a bad fright this morning over our rooms. He will get a worse shaking at his soul before the day is out. Let me see, we have something under two hours before boarding our ship, and I have some work to do at the inn before then."

"Our ship?" asked the bewildered Mipps.

Syn laughed. "You have ever the taste for piracy, my good Mipps. Well, here I find Black Nick obliging enough to build us a ship for that purpose.

Between us we managed to take Black Satan's Sulphur Pit, and with some luck and skill we'll now take Black Nick's St. Nicholas." After a gentle ride to kill the time required for an imagined interview at the Governor's House, they galloped back into town that their horses should appear in a fine lather. Re-entering the inn, Syn called for pens and paper, and in the privacy of his room settled down to writing carefully, while Mipps sat smoking and watching.

Presently Syn remarked, "'Tis a good thing remembering what a man's handwriting is like. I recollect Black Nick's very well. This paper we may not need at all, but it is best to be prepared. I wish you to sign your name here as witness, beneath this signature of the Governor's clerk. Black Nick has already put his name, as you see." Mipps grinned and signed, then added, "How do you know there's a Governor's clerk?"

"Because the Governor is Spanish and therefore lazy. Of course he would have a clerk. This document makes it quite clear that Black Nick has made over his ship to me. Very kind, I swear. He states, too, that I have paid for it in full.

Now let us take a boat and a closer look at the St. Nicholas." Saying which, Syn placed the paper in his pocket, led the way out on to the quay and engaged a boat. It was then mid afternoon with a fine breeze blowing.

"Just the weather for sailing, and like old times, Master Carpenter," said Syn cheerfully. "She is a fine ship by the looks of her. We must give her designer his due. She seems fit to withstand heavy weather, in that she could cut through it. A fine length of mast too, all three of them. And a fine stretch of canvas she can carry. I long to stretch my sea legs on her decks. I think she'll ride very prettily, Mister Mipps."

"I think so, too, sir," replied Mipps, looking up with great admiration at the black hull brightened with brass cannon. "A frigate of fifty guns, I take her."

"Aye, and she's capable of a lot," added Syn. "Heavy work; light work; quick work."

"And dirty work," grinned Mipps.

Grasping the rope-ladder alongside from the tossing boat, Syn, followed by Mipps, climbed aboard, and was received at the gangway by Tarragona.

"Ship ready for sea?" asked Syn.

"All ready, Captain Clegg," the officer answered.

"Then pipe all hands on deck. I have something to say to the men for their advantage," and Syn, swaggering to the companion ladder, climbed up to the poop-deck and leaned upon the rail.

Meanwhile from rigging and holds the crew swarmed on to the main-deck beneath him and stood staring at the magnificent stranger who had boasted to be their friend.

"All on deck, sir," said an officer.

"All on deck, sir," repeated Tarragona.

"Then bring me the ships' sailing papers," ordered Syn.

Tarragona brought him the papers from his cabin under the poop. Under the eyes of the crew Syn unfolded them, read them, and frowned. Then, folding them again, he handed them to Mipps, who stood on duty beside him and produced the document which he had forged at the inn. This he read through carefully and then let it trail over the rail from his hand so that all could see.

"My lads," he said, "I have had a serious difference over this voyage with Black Nick. The unfair way in which he has kept you aboard while he drinks with the Governor infuriated me. Although he has engaged a pirate crew, he had no intention of hoisting the black flag. Well, we are going to hoist it now, and if Black Nick thinks we are going to escort treasure-ships tamely to Spain, he is mightily mistaken. That treasure will be more valuable to us, when we lock our own share in our own sea-chests. Though I have taken over the ship from him, he still expects me to wait for him so that he and his family may have a free passage to Havana. His chests are aboard, but we must wait till it pleases him to finish his drunken bout with the Governor. We'll have a look at these chests. They shall be your first prize. Now who is for joining under new articles better than ever you signed yet, I promise you? If any refuse, he is at liberty to swim for the harbour before we sail, and no harm done. I take it none of you are pirates for the fun of the thing, though I promise you many a merry time when duty's done. No, like myself, you are pirates in order to get rich quickly. Hard work and dangers, and then money to spend ashore like gentlemen. Now, I know that I am the man for you, and you the men for me. It was I, Captain Clegg, who killed Black Satan, the notorious but hated negro captain, in fair fight. With the help of this gallant sea-dog by my side, my master carpenter, I captured his pirate vessel, the Sulphur Pit, and filled her with the treasures from our prizes. As then, I promise you that I'll be first to board any ship we think is worth the taking, and, if you wish, I'll prove my swordsmanship against any three you care to match against me.

But why spill our blood when we want other's treasure? No, let's serve out double grog, and then to sea. What say you?"

At this the whole crew fell to cheering, and when a great barrel of rum was tapped, their enthusiasm knew no bounds.

Drinking as heavily as any, Syn then shouted, "Bring tools to prise open Black Nick's chests. And now, my lads, though he never meant to hoist it, no doubt there's a Jolly Roger in the flag locker? If so, let's hoist it to show our true colours and our teeth." One of the crew cried out that they had one below which they had planned to hoist if Black Nick wished it or no.

"Fetch it," cried Syn heartily. "You'll have no cause to mutiny now." At once a great black flag was produced by the crew, with a white skull-andcrossbones painted upon it.

"Splendid!" cried Syn. "Mister Tarragona, since our course is nor' east, we shall pass in sight of the Governor's House, where Black Nick drinks and laughs at our waiting for him. Keep your eyes skinned, sir, and when we are abreast of it strike the St. Nicholas and run up that Jolly Roger. At the same time let 'em have a Governor's salute. Aye, a broadside of the lee-guns, and see there's shot in 'em. Now, my lads, put a deck stopper on the cable, and then cut the cable abaft it. Hoist the jib and when I sing out, stand by to slip. Shake a leg, my jolly dogs. Topsail halyards. Stand by to slip. Slip the cable. Hoist away." Then he broke into his chanty in a ringing voice:

"Oh, here's to the feet what have walked the plank, Yo-ho for the dead man's throttle And here's to the corpses afloat in the tank And the dead man's teeth in the bottle."

With the running of ropes, the rattle of running blocks, the crack of filling canvas, and with the straining of every plank, the St. Nicholas leapt through the waves in obedience to her new master.

Chapter 16. The Red-Bearded Planter

In the Governor's House, His Spanish Excellency and his guests, Black Nick and a great giant, with a luxuriant red beard of Scottish descent, he boasted, called McCallum at that time, played cards and drank. Black Nick's wife, the beautiful Imogene Almago, was forced to make the fourth, but since the gentlemen were drunk, she came in for little blame in playing carelessly. Her attention was listless for the cards, but riveted upon a handsome, slim boy who slept upon a sofa. She was disgusted with these so-called gentlemen, when the very cards she had to handle were wet with red wine.

Suddenly a thunderous crash of thunder shook the house, bringing them all to their feet, and partly sobering the men.

The screaming of the Governor's slaves brought them out upon the balcony facing the sea. There they saw the white seawall of the garden was shattered.

The Governor's pleasure sailing boat was sinking. The private quay had crumbled, and a great swift ship was passing close in-shore.

"It is my ship," cried Black Nick. "See the flag, St. Nicholas."

"They are hauling it down," said the red-bearded planter.

"And running up the Black Flag. Pirates!" shouted the Governor.

"Oh God, Nicholas," sobbed Imogene. "It is Christopher. I know it."

"Nonsense!" replied Nicholas. "How could it be?" But the proof was soon to come, for an empty treasure-chest was thrown overboard, and across the water they heard a ringing voice cry out in Spanish, "As for these things, heave 'em overboard and let 'em float ashore to her. I'll have no petticoats aboard my ship." They saw a magnificent figure in scarlet stooping over another chest upon the high poop-deck, and hurling garments over the bulwarks into the sea. The tide was running towards shore, and as the ship under full sail disappeared around the head, laces, satins, velvets and rich brocades came floating to the beach. A little boy was highly delighted in retrieving them.

"Look, Mother, another of your dresses. I remember this one well. And look, here is yet one more of your mantillas." That night

Black Nick fled in panic, leaving his wife and son behind in a convent, promising the Lady Mother large sums of money on his return. He shipped aboard a pirate vessel in which he was interested, and sailed for the North American coast. He abandoned all hope of recovering the St. Nicholas, and only thought of escaping from Doctor Syn.

The red-bearded planter did not take things so tamely. Foreseeing the danger of losing his treasure ships that were awaiting the St. Nicholas, he took horse and rode the long way up the island towards the Gulf of Batabano. But the way was harder than the way of the St. Nicholas, and he arrived to hear sad news. He found the captain of the Santa Mariana sick in his cabin and with a fine tale to tell.

"We were signalled by the St. Nicholas to put to sea as arranged. When out of sight of land we two captains were signalled to come aboard the St.

Nicholas. The Captain Clegg, who had command, ordered us to fetch our treasure-chests and hand them over to his keeping, for, as he said, should we fall in with enemy ships, he could outsail them and save the treasure-chests for the King of Spain. I was glad to do this, and to be relieved thus of my responsibility, but my colleague thought otherwise, and refused to give over his charge. Captain Clegg raged at this, but eventually ordered the voyage to proceed. About an hour later the St. Nicholas dropped astern, for she had been sailing between us. She then came up again rapidly upon the lee side of the Celesta, and without warning opened a broadside which completely crippled her. I could not retaliate, since my colleague was between us sheltering the traitor, so I turned and ran for the Gulf, thus at least saving my men and your ship. As we tacked away, we saw Clegg's men board Celesta, and after taking away her treasure to boats, they deliberately sank her. I think that every man aboard the unfortunate vessel perished."

"I'll have this Clegg hanged as a pirate, if I spend all my fortune in the doing it," cried the planter. "He will not hide from me." But Clegg had no intention of hiding. After robbing and sinking three fat merchant ships bound for Cuba, he sailed back to Santiago, sank a ship in the harbour mouth in passing, and then as a warning once more shattered the garden wall of the Governor's house which was being rebuilt. He then rowed ashore and impudently demanded twenty thousand pieces of gold, or he vowed he'd destroy the town. He also ordered the Governor to hand over Black Nick to his keeping.

The Governor raised the money by the next day, but assured Clegg that Black Nick had gone—with the planter, he thought—and was no doubt in Havana. So with the money in his hold, Clegg sailed for Havana.

After sending a broadside into the astonished and terrified town, he once more made his impudent demand for payment, threatening to destroy the town and shipping if the money was not forthcoming within six hours.

Now, McCallum, the planter, being one of the richest men in all Havana, was summoned to the Citadel for consultation with the Governor. He was no coward, and had not the same dread of Clegg as Nicholas. He was not the type who runs away to save his skin. His fury against Clegg added to his bravery, and he now saw a heaven-sent chance for settling his score.

"We will collect this money, and I will carry it aboard," he told the Governor. "I will then lure him to my house on the plantation, under the pretext of delivering Black Nick into his hands. I will tell him of his enemy's fear of him, and the thought of suddenly meeting him and settling his account will be too good to resist. He will come, and as we dine we will have a strong guard of military to arrest him. Then we will demand full payment, and hang the lot of the rascals after it is paid." They discussed the plan in detail, and that evening McCallum was rowed aboard the St. Nicholas.

As the boat swung beneath the lofty hull, he saw that the name of it was being changed. Painters were busily at work on slung rigging. As he read the new name he chuckled to himself.

"This Clegg is a devilish rascal. He thinks things out well. And so do I. It takes a Scot to beat an Englishman. He'll find I am the greater devil yet."

And Syn had thought things out well, for the name of the ship was now the Imogene.

Chapter 17. Clegg's "Imogene"

Having paid over the ransom for the town in Clegg's cabin on the Imogene, McCallum came straight to the point with the most villainous frankness. He told Clegg, quite engagingly, that he had no love for Black Nick, and would give a lot to see him badly frightened before being killed. He then asked casually:

"How do you propose killing him?" Syn answered: "I shall force him to utter my name, Clegg. It is the sound a man will make when he is strangled. And I think I shall kill him with my bare hands. Then no doubt I shall dig out his heart with that harpoon upon the cabin wall, behind you."

"You must hate the man vastly to be so bloodthirsty," laughed the planter.

"I hate him enough," replied Syn.

The next day, according to their arrangements, Syn was rowed ashore to the plantation beach. The planter was there to meet him, and the boat's crew were left guarding the boat, for, as the planter pointed out, should too many men appear, Black Nick would become suspicious.

Now, Clegg's crew had told him that they feared a trap would be set for their captain, and asked permission to stand by to rescue him. Knowing that McCallum could be no friend to him, though he hated Black Nick the worse, Syn was alert for any treachery, but seeing in the air an opportunity to impress his men with his utter disregard for danger, and somehow trusting in his own destiny, which always whispered to him that he would eventually kill Nicholas, he did not care, but walked gaily with McCallum through the woods to the house. This was a large wooden bungalow, built high upon a slope, the back of which afforded a dry store for cattle fodder. It was a hot day, and by the time they entered the front verandah they were ready for food and drink. But Syn resolved that there would be no food or drink for him in that house. Black Nick's capture was what he had come for, and that would be more than meat and wine. He was chancing no drugging from McCallum's hospitality. They entered a spacious living-room, with table laid for three.

"That is Black Nick's usual seat," said the host. "If you sit there opposite, with your back to the door, he will not see you in that high-backed chair. The lazy devil is always late, so we will sit down now, and I will send a servant to tell him dinner is served. Then you may do what you like. You may prefer to kill a man before or after dinner. I suggest after, for personally I am hungry. So long as you do kill him, it's of no odds to me."

"I shall be obliged if you will send for him," said Syn, taking his seat, while McCallum ordered one of the servants to fetch Black Nick.

Syn heard the door open behind him, and a heavy step care round the table.

Although he was alive to treachery, Syn never doubted but that this was Black Nick, and he was something astonished to see confronting him a Spanish officer fully armed.

"I arrest you, sir, in the name of the Governor of Havana for piracy on the high seas. Come in, there." A tramp of feet behind him made Syn glance quickly behind him to see a file of guards.

McCallum laughed. "It is quite true, Captain Clegg, that Black Nick is afraid of you. So much that he ran away to sea as a pirate rather than fight you to recover his ship which you stole so cleverly. But I am a man of different kidney. You do not steal my ships and treasure and go scot free. No, you shall hang on Havana docks."

"So the Governor of Santiago lied to me when he said that Black Nick was with you in Havana," said Syn calmly.

"Of course he did," laughed the planter. "May not a Governor lie to a thief?"

"So much the worse for the Governor of Santiago," replied Syn.

"Come, sir," said the officer. "My men wait to escort you to the Town."

"You had best hand over your sword," said the planter.

"And let us get clear before his men know of this and attempt a rescue." Syn rose and drew his sword, but had no intention of handing it to the officer. The twelve guards behind him were cavalry men with drawn sabres. As he was quickly weighing up his chances, he noticed blue smoke curling along between the floor-boards. He also heard an ominous crackling of burning wood, and felt a strange heat under his soles.

"I can assure you that my men will rescue me," he said. "Oh yes. Alive or dead. If dead, God help your town. They will spare nothing."

"That is for us to prevent," replied the officer haughtily.

As he spoke he staggered back for a flame leapt up through

the floor and caught the table-cloth, while screams of "Fire" echoed through the house. But that was not so terrifying as the half-naked red figure which dashed into the room and with a double swing of a tomahawk severed the necks of the two soldiers nearest to Syn, and then leapt upon the table in the midst of the flames crying out "Shuhshuhgah".

"Shuhshuhgah," echoed Syn with a mighty laugh, as he drove his sword through the neck of another soldier.

"I scalp you. You good enough. You officer," cried the Redskin, swinging a blow at the captain of the Guard.

The planter dashed for the safety of the verandah, and jumping the rails to the grass below, ran for the woods, while Syn drove the frightened soldiers before him with his sword. And then with a shout the faithful Mipps, having disregarded orders, rushed through the smoke at the head of his boat's crew.

The soldiers broke and ran with the pirates after them, and as Syn rushed for the verandah he saw Shuhshuhgah in the blinding smoke calmly scalping the dead officer. Before he could finish this operation, Syn had dragged him clear of the burning house.

"I fired the house," said the Redskin. "Heard that officer talk last night about the trap for you. Came up to join you. Saw fodder under floor. Fired it.

Easy."

"Back to the boats, and we'll talk when on the ship," said Syn.

That night the pirates sacked Havana, seized the Governor and hanged him on the docks where he had planned to hang Clegg. They then set sail for Santiago, "for I'll have no Governor of a mere town lying to me," cried Clegg.

So was Santiago sacked and another Governor hanged.

A suitable island was found for their treasures to be hidden in, and for the careening of the Imogene, and from his secret base they sailed and sailed again, taking their toll of ship after ship. Even pirate ships were not secure from them.

Indeed, the crew noted that their Captain attacked these with the greater spirit, for on one of them he always hoped to meet with Nicholas.

Chapter 18. Mutiny

During the twelve years or so that the Imogene kept the seas and ruled them, there were few Governments interested in shipping who had not posted large rewards for her captain. But Clegg and his loyal rascals went on plundering and outwitting all their enemies. All those years he had counted upon the good faith of his crew. Believing in each man, who, to his profit, had sailed so long with him, he had only once been troubled with mutiny. On that occasion, off Anastasia, he ran the ringleader through the neck in fair fight. He heard no more of it after that. The only other case of treachery was the negro who stole his Virgil, thinking it a book of magic, and deserted. Against this he had had twelve years of faithful service, until a mysterious discontent arose, and he demanded explanation.

"This ship is haunted by a devil," faltered a spokesman. "He speaks to us in the night watches, warning us against you for our safety. He says you once blew up your own ship, sacrificing all to steal their treasure. He says you will do it again to us." Mipps answered this. "Clegg never blew up his own ship in his life. You might as well accuse me of such a thing. Who is this funny croaker?"

"He comes at night from the hold, like a stowaway, and we fear him," replied the man nervously. "He says we must maroon the captain or die."

"I'll have neither ghost, devil nor stowaway aboard my ship unless he signs our articles," cried Syn. "Down to the hold, you dog, and rout him out. I have a wish to see this devil face to face."

"Here, and you remember me. I speak now." Syn turned at the dreadful voice behind him, and faced the mulatto. He recognized him at once as the sole survivor of the Sulphur Pit. Immediately the rascal began to prophesy dreadful things against the ship and crew unless they disposed of their captain by making him walk the plank or by marooning.

"Seize him and lash him to the mast," cried Syn.

Shuhshuhgah and Mipps were on him in a second, and Syn helped them bind him to the mainmast.

"Give me your scalping-knife, and I'll cut the rascal's lying tongue out," he cried.

Shuhshuhgah drew his knife and forced the mulatto's mouth open.

"I'll do my own dirty work," said Syn.

"I am so skilled at it," answered the Redskin.

To the astonished and terrified crew there seemed to be three quick movements of the Indian's arm, and three things fell behind him on the deck. A tongue cut out at the root, and two severed ears.

"No talk. No hear," said the Indian grimly.

Mipps picked up the grisly objects and threw them overboard.

"Make for that coral reef. We'll put him ashore there," said Syn.

He cut the man's bonds, and ordered a boat to be lowered. It was Mipps and the Indian who went with him, while Syn kept the ship, facing his cowed crew.

"That's the uncharted reef where the tide rises fathoms deep," said one of them.

"It will be the more merciful," said Syn. "Water and sharks." They watched the marooning in silence, every man aboard. When the boat was once more hoisted, and Mipps with Shuhshuhgah were aboard, the crew pushed forward Pete, the Chinese cook, to be their spokesman. He stammered out that they wished to put the ship back, so that they could rescue the marooned man. In a blind rage, Clegg snatched a marine-spike from Mipps, and broke the yellow dog's back with it. Pete fell dead upon the deck, and as Mipps and Shuhshuhgah tossed him overboard the mad captain, with drawn sword, drove the men to the rigging as he roared:

"Get up aloft, you dogs. Cram on the canvas. Every stitch. I'll have no mutiny aboard my ship. No, nor devils neither, other than myself." The ship leapt on through the lashing foam, while the sinister wailing of the marooned man's tongueless voice echoed in the rigging, and long after he had disappeared below the skyline they all seemed to see his tall, weird figure rising up into the sky and following the ship. But Syn saw more. Wherever he looked into the waters, he had to shut his eyes against the grinning face of yellow Pete.

Chapter 19. The Mulatto

From the South Seas and the coral reef they sailed for weeks on end towards their harbourage. Not only the crew, but Clegg himself thought of nothing but the horror of that marooning. Save on duty, Clegg kept to his cabin.

He seemed dazed. On one occasion he called Mipps and whispered:

"Look at my forearm, here above the wrist. I was never tattooed in all my life, and yet there is the picture of a man walking the plank with a shark beneath. How came this symbol here?"

"I done it for you," said Mipps—"that night at Santiago, after we'd sacked the town. You and me was drinking, and I never see you drunk before. You ordered me to do it with the help of Yellow Pete, the cook."

"I can see Pete's face looking up at me dead from the sea, always," whispered Syn. "It was a fault, this tattooing. A man can be identified so easily by that, and I have suddenly no wish to be known as Clegg. Nicholas is tattooed from head to foot. I have driven him round and round the world, and he has fled because he could be so easily identified. Now I am in like case, for I am followed by the dead hulk of that mulatto. So long as I sail ships, so long will he be following in the wake. If I give up my chase of Nicholas, perhaps that haunting corpse will give up chasing me. I always feel him following the ship, just as I always see Yellow Pete's face in the waters. 'Tis bad enough to be shadowed by a living man, as Nicholas has been; but to be followed by a corpse is too much to endure. Where can I hide from it?"

"Dymchurch-under-the-Wall," whispered Mipps. "Go back there as parson and thank God for a whole skin. Maybe I will go there one day too, but now for your sake, sir, it's better if we separate. Shuhshuhgah and myself have spoke of it. We can hide up your tracks. I take your sea-chest and stow it safe in Boston, where you can book passage for England. You must get to Boston by way of the Redskins' country. You and the long-missing Shuhshuhgah, returning like the prodigals, after years of preaching the 'Oly Gospel to the savages."

"And give up my vengeance?" asked Syn.

"You may as easily catch Black Nick there as on the high seas of the world," said Mipps. "Besides, he may be dead, same as he said his wife was when he wrote and pleaded with you for mercy."

"I'll not believe she's dead," said Syn. "He is a proved liar. When he sent me that letter some years ago, I knew it in my heart he lied. I think even yet I'll reckon with them both. Aye, perhaps at Dymchurch."

Many months later, Doctor Syn, with the Redskin's help, rejoined Mipps in Boston. By this time he had begun to think that Nicholas must be dead.

"So all that is left to me," he said, "is Romney Marsh and quiet years. But will the past rise up against me even there?"

"Not so far as the pirates is concerned," replied Mipps. "And let me tell you, sir, the Imogene ain't the first ship to have gone to Davy Jones' Locker through a piece of carelessness in the powder magazine."

"Have you done that again?" demanded Syn.

Mipps looked offended. "I'm a 'one-man servant', I am, sir, and dead pirates tell no tales."

"All of them?" asked Syn.

Mipps nodded. "Every man aboard. And no deaf mutes this time swimming about neither. A thorough job I made of it, believe me, sir."

"God rest their souls!" said the parson piously.

"Amen," relied Mipps with equal piety.

Doctor Syn sadly shook his head.

Mipps winked.

Chapter 20. The Return

Mervyn Ransom, master and owner of the brig City of London, trading between New England and the Port of London, had a great liking for his passenger, Doctor Syn. He respected this quiet scholar who had given up so many years in the service of Christianity amongst the Indian tribes. The voyage was uneventful till the reached at last the Channel. There they ran into the greatest storm the south coast had seen for many a year, and as they drove along towards the Kent coast, the captain of the ship began to give up hope. It was then that he loved Doctor Syn. This parson was first up aloft to trim sails, and had it not been for some uncanny knowledge of the coast which came back to him across the years, they would have run foul of Dungeness. And then the fire broke out in the hold. The heat was unbearable, the waves terrific. The ship was being driven on to Dymchurch Wall.

"'Tis a short cut to my destination," cried the parson. "There's nothing left but to jump for it." With a long cord lashed to his precious sea-chest and tied to his wrist, Syn toppled his worldly belongings over the ship's side, just as the brig was heading for destruction. The chest landed on the sand beneath the driving waves, and then Syn and the captain jumped after the crew, and as they battled with the monster waves, the wind and waters sang in Syn's ear:

"Here's to the feet what have walked the plank, Yo-ho for the dead man's throttle, And here's to the corpses afloat in the tank And the dead man's teeth in the bottle."

Ingram Content Group UK Ltd.
Milton Keynes UK
UKHW011109310323
419466UK00004B/94